KASSY O'ROARKE

TREASURE HUNTER

KASSY O'ROARKE

TREASURE HUNTER

PET DETECTIVE MYSTERIES
BOOK TWO

KELLY OLIVER

—Beaver's Pond Press—
Minneapolis, MN

PRAISE FOR *KASSY O'ROARKE, CUB REPORTER,* PET DETECTIVE MYSTERIES BOOK ONE

"A juicy middle-grade mystery in which a young investigator learns that it's okay to be vulnerable."

—*Foreword Reviews*

"A polished, convincing, kid-centered adventure, with endearing characters and a strong sense of middle-school humor. Oliver writes in a breezy, kid-friendly style that's perfect for early middle schoolers, who will easily identity with Kassy. A strong series debut!"

—*BlueInk Review*

"An action-packed and exciting adventure mystery novel. *Kassy O'Roarke, Cub Reporter* is well-written and likely to entertain both animal and mystery lovers of all ages. It's most highly recommended!"

—Jeff Mangus, *Readers' Favorite*

"A whole lot of fun—and delivers in every way an adventure story should! The mystery's twists and turns are clever and unpredictable, but Kelly Oliver builds more than a detailed mystery. She also creates a heartwarming world populated with believable characters who feel like people you know."

—Sarah Scheele, *Readers' Favorite*

"Great fun, with its underpants-wearing animals and many memorable characters, like Flatulent Freddie the farting ferret. The book is action-packed, and the characters are all likable and realistic, with relatable problems. The plot has twists and turns that are sure to keep readers on their toes. I was hooked by the first page!"

—Kristen Van Campen (teen reviewer), *Readers' Favorite*

"This is a purely enjoyable adventure filled with memorable characters, an endearing protagonist, and a lot of heart."

—US Review of Books

"For everyone who's into adventure, mystery, and a whole bunch of middle-grade fun, this first in series does the trick! Beware, you won't want to set this book down anytime soon."

—Chanticleer Reviews

Edited by Paige Polinsky

Illustrated by BNP Design Studio

Production editor: Hanna Kjeldbjerg

Cover illustration by BNP Design Studio

ISBN 13: 978-1-64343-864-1

Book design by Athena Currier

Beaver's Pond Press
939 West Seventh Street
Saint Paul, MN 55402

(952) 829-8818

www.BeaversPondPress.com

To order, visit www.kellyoliverbooks.com. Reseller discounts available.

For media inquiries, please call or e-mail Kelly Oliver at kellyoliverbooks@gmail.com. For more information, visit www.kellyoliverbooks.com.

For all the quarantined kids . . .

1

SHIH TZU PUPPY! YARA IS MISSING

THE DOGGIE BEAUTY SALON REEKS OF strawberries and dog breath. I guess the berry-scented shampoo is supposed to cover up the dog breath, but instead the place smells like a rotten waffle. I scrunch up my nose as I examine two leashes attached to a stainless steel arm overhead. I run my fingers across the smooth, cool surface as I circle the table. Yara was last seen yesterday standing on this table, waiting for a bow to be tied around her black-and-white topknot. The contraption looks more like a torture table than a grooming table. The black poodle on the next table over is enjoying her buzz cut . . . either that, or, with the leash around her neck, the strap around her belly, and the muzzle over her mouth, her furiously wagging tail is the only weapon she's got left to hit the groomer.

"You went to the back room to get a bow, and when you came back out, Yara was gone?" I ask the groomer. I write everything she says in my little green notebook. She's a round woman dressed all in pink with white canvas sneakers. Even her poofy hair is pink, which makes it look like cotton candy.

My name is Kassy and I'm thirteen. Okay, my whole name is Kassandra Urania O'Roarke, and I'm actually twelve, but I'll be thirteen in forty-two days. I just opened a pet detective

business yesterday. This is my first case—unless you count Apollo, the cougar cub my pesky little brother hid in an old shed. My brother's name is Perseus Charon O'Roarke, but I call him Crispy because he almost burned the barn down last year. He's eight, but sometimes he acts like a big baby. My new step-sister Ronny lost her Shi Tzu, Yara. She thought her puppy escaped from their apartment. She didn't know Dad had taken the dog to the groomer. It was a double-blow to discover the puppy was missing from the groomer's too.

Holding a wire-tooth comb in her mouth, the groomer nods as she swipes another swath of curls off the poodle's back.

"Did you see who took her?" I glance around to confirm there are three ways out of the room: a wooden door, presumably leading to the back room where they store the bows, and a glass door leading into a pet store. A pair of automatic sliding glass doors lead to the parking lot.

The groomer takes the comb from her mouth. "Nope. I came back and she was gone."

"Was anyone else working here at the time?"

"Sarah, but she was taking her lunch break." Candy, the groomer points to a glass booth, where a wiry woman is brushing out a fluffy Persian cat.

I make a note: *Question Sarah.*

"Was anyone else in the shop? Other dog owners?"

"You'll have to ask Sarah." Candy shrugs.

I put a star in my notebook next to *Question Sarah.*

"Did anyone not show up for their appointment? Maybe they came in, saw Yara, and took her."

Cotton-candy gives me a quizzical look. "Ask Sarah."

"Did you hear the door jingle while you were in the back?"

She shakes her head. "But I had my earbuds in."

"Are there any competing businesses nearby? A competitor who would want to make you look bad by stealing your clients?"

The groomer scrunches her eyebrows. "I don't know."

"How about unhappy employees? Someone who might have a grudge against the pet shop?"

"Freddie found something!" My little brother, Crispy, is crawling around on all fours following his ferret, Flatulent Freddie. (Yeah . . . he farts a lot.) Freddie sniffs a sparkly dot winking up from the floor.

I go over to investigate. Taking a pair of tweezers from my spy vest, I pick up the tiny jewel and drop it into a Ziplock baggie. I always carry extra baggies in my vest for collecting evidence. My spy vest is really one of my dad's old fishing vests with loads of pockets for holding my equipment: magnifying glass, notebook, pen, fingerprint powder, Scotch tape (good for lifting fingerprints), and an emergency granola bar. The vest has one big pocket across the back where I keep the walkie-talkie my friend Butler gave me. Butler's mom owns Patel Pastries, the bakery where we have our pet detective headquarters.

When Crispy stops crawling and sits up, Freddie jumps up on his shoulder and curls around his neck. My brother never goes anywhere without farting Freddie. Crispy looks up at me with his catlike green eyes. "What is it?"

I hold up the baggie to the light and study the pink jewel. "I don't know . . . yet."

"Is it important?" Crispy asks.

"You never know what might be important." I stuff the baggie into one of my vest pockets. "That's why you have to pay attention to every clue, no matter how insignificant it seems."

"Kassy?" My brother stands up, his ferret clinging to his head. "Freddie says he's hungry."

I roll my eyes. Crispy still insists the animals talk to him. Ever since Dad moved out last year, Crispy hears animal voices. To be fair, we do have a petting zoo at home, and Mom is a veterinarian.

"You mean *you're* hungry."

Crispy nods.

"Here." I hand him my month-old emergency granola bar. Since school got out for the summer, we don't have our regular lunchtime anymore.

Crispy unwraps it, breaks it into three parts, and hands one piece to Freddie, who grabs it in both paws and starts nibbling. "Want some?" he asks Ronny, who is rocking back and forth in the corner hugging her soccer ball and crying. Ronny's real name is Veronica. She's sort of like my stepsister, but not really since her mom and my dad aren't married . . . yet. I'm still hoping Dad sees the light and decides to come back home.

"You kids should probably go outside to play," Cotton Candy says.

"Come on, you two." I head for the exit.

"Three," Crispy corrects me. "Don't forget Freddie."

On the way out the door, I remember one more important question and turn back. "What time did Yara go missing?" Ronny's shih tzu puppy is black-and-white and rips up everything in the house, including my legs. I don't know why anyone would want to steal her.

"Sarah was out at lunch, so it must have been between noon and one." The groomer gives the poodle a dog biscuit.

Between noon and one. That was during the awards ceremony when I was a runner-up for the Thompson Award for Journalism from our middle school's newspaper. My next story is going to be front-page news. And next year, I'm going to win the award.

"This has never happened before." The groomer attaches a tiny purple bow to the poodle's topknot. "I'm so sorry. Please apologize again to Miss Mari."

"Kassy will find her!" Ronny sniffles, spinning her soccer ball on her index finger. Ronny is a whiz with a soccer ball. "She's a pet detective."

"And a reporter," Crispy chimes in.

Freddie just toots his two cents' worth.

I shake my head and wave my hand back and forth in front of my face.

Outside, Ronny's mother is waiting in the minivan.

I hop into the passenger seat and Ronny, Crispy, and Freddie pile into the back. I get the front since I'm the oldest. Maybe when I turn thirteen, Mom will finally let me have a cell phone. Ronny has one, and she's only ten.

"Where's Yara?" Mari asks. She sounds upset. Mari is Ronny's mom. Unlike my mom, she always has perfectly painted fingernails and wears matching red lipstick. When she found out Yara went missing from the beauty parlor, she went ballistic and had a big fight with the groomer. That's why she sent me in to ask questions today. She was afraid of what she might do to the groomer.

"What happened?" Mari asks.

"We found this." I pull the baggie out of my pocket.

"Let me see that." Mari holds out her manicured hand. She wants us to call her "Mom," but I refuse.

Ronny and Crispy are playing tug-of-war with the soccer ball.

"Quit roughhousing back there," Mari says as she takes the baggie. "This could be a rhinestone from Yara's collar." She gives it back to me. "Buckle your seatbelts. Next stop, FedEx to make copies of the flyer."

The flyer offers a reward and has a picture of Yara, her little shih tzu tongue hanging out of her smiling puppy face. She's wearing a pink ribbon in her topknot, and the black-and-white hair on her head stands straight up, shooting out from her skull like a fountain. Her bushy tail looks like a pom-pom. I have to admit, she's pretty cute.

An hour later, we're going block by block, putting up flyers in the neighborhood around the pet store, which is just six blocks from Dad's town house.

"Why would someone steal Yara?" I ask, stapling another flyer to a telephone pole.

Ronny stops bouncing her soccer ball. "Maybe she just got loose and she's hiding."

"Well, she didn't open the door to the beauty salon on her own." I push down on the stapler.

Tears well in Ronny's amber eyes. "You've got to find Yara," she whimpers. "I love her. She's my best friend." *Oh no!* She's crying again.

I grimace. Seeing other people cry makes me want to cry, too. But detectives don't cry. "Don't worry. We'll find her." *At least, I hope we'll find her.* Across the street, I glimpse another flyer taped to a streetlight.

"Don't cry, sweetie." Mari puts her arm around Ronny. "She's got to be someplace close by."

Not necessarily. Not if someone stole her and already sold her. I keep my scary thoughts to myself.

I look both ways and then dash across the street.

"Kassandra!" Mari yells. "What are you doing?"

I cringe. "Just a minute."

Wait. There are three squares of paper attached to the pole. I stare at the flyers. *Holy hijack!* Three dogs are missing. One has a wrinkly face and a corkscrew tail, the second has shaggy bangs covering his dark eyes, and the third looks like a fox. *Could there be a dognapper at work? Really, how could four dogs go missing from this neighborhood?* Each flyer offers a reward for the return of the dog, no questions asked. I take out my notebook, do a quick sketch of each pup, and jot down the information.

If I've learned one thing as a journalist, there are always a lot of questions to be asked. And, usually, there are a lot more questions than answers.

A car honks as I run back across the street.

"Kassandra, you have to be more careful, *mijita*." Mari scrunches her eyebrows. "You're in the city now."

It's true. Downtown Nashville is nothing like where Mom lives, out in Lemontree Heights. Here, the streets are crowded with parked cars, five-story condo buildings, and couples

zipping by on electric scooters. It's been over a year now since Dad moved into the city, and I'm still not used to all the noise and lack of trees. I don't know why Dad doesn't just come back to the farm, where you can hear the crickets singing and the air smells like grass.

Here, the aroma of fried onions from a Greek restaurant mixes with car exhaust and the stinky perfume of strangers. At home, even the earthy scents of the petting zoo are comforting. And I bet no one in Lemontree Heights would steal a dog and sell it.

After an hour of posting flyers, I'm hot and sweaty. My face is on fire. I turn beet red and burn up if I get too much sun. "I'm dying of thirst." I lean against a telephone pole, fanning myself with a handful of flyers. It's only June and already hot as blazes.

"Let's get you home for some lemonade and cookies." Mari is always trying to bribe me with homemade cookies and coconut flan. If she thinks she can win me over with yummy desserts, she has another thing coming. Crispy, the little traitor, may fall for it. But not me. Although I have to admit, it does sound pretty good. The only cookies Mom makes are gluten-free health cookies with zucchini or carrot or some other vegetable hidden inside. As if I won't realize they're laced with produce. Mom's cookies taste like dog biscuits. That's why Freddie and Crispy love them.

Back at Dad's town house, it takes all my willpower to resist Mari's chocolate chip cookies. I submit to the lemonade out of necessity and drink down two full glasses in a matter of minutes. Zeus, our golden retriever, follows us into the den.

Dad got custody of Zeus, and Mom got me and Crispy. Zeus's tail beats against my brother's leg, and the dog lifts his face and touches noses with Freddie.

Ronny whips her phone out of her jeans pocket and snaps a picture. "For my Instagram."

Mom would have kittens if she found out Ronny was posting pictures of Crispy or me on Instagram. Dad calls Mom a *Luddite*, which means she resists using new technologies. But Mom doesn't care if she's living in the dark ages. Instead, she owns it. Even in her vet's office, Mom always says, "My hands and eyes know more than that X-ray machine."

In the den, I settle into an overstuffed leather chair. Ronny turns on the television . . . something else we don't get much of at home. Rotten Ronny can watch as much TV as she wants. Crispy and Freddie munch on a cookie while Ronny flips through the channels.

I take out my notebook and review the evidence in Yara's case. First, she was taken—or escaped—from the doggie beauty salon yesterday between noon and one in the afternoon. Second, she is not wearing any bows or ribbons. Third, what is possibly a rhinestone from her collar was found on the floor of the salon. I make a note: *Is she wearing her collar now?* Most likely, she is wearing her collar, given that it was not at the salon. Maybe Yara wriggled to get away from the thief, and in the struggle lost a jewel from her collar. Fourth, her picture with a reward is now plastered all over the neighborhood. Fifth, there are at least three other dogs missing.

I tap my pen on the notebook. *Could Cotton Candy or her partner in crime, Sarah, have dognapped Yara?* The groomer said this was the first time a dog had gone missing from her shop. *Should I believe her?* You learn as a reporter and as a detective not to take everything everybody says at face value. Always corroborate every story. I start a list of possible suspects. My list isn't very long since I have so few leads. *Sigh.* I doodle a picture of the puppy on my notebook. The most likely explanation for four dogs missing from the same neighborhood at the same time is a dognapping ring.

"Guess what?" Mari appears in the doorway, a smile cracking her face. "Someone found Yara!"

Crispy turns to me. "But Kassy was going to find her."

"They saw the flyer." Mari claps her hands together.

Ronny jumps up and down. "Yay! Yara's coming home!"

"I'm going to call your dad and tell him to go to the bank and get the reward money, then pick up Yara on his way home." Mari taps on her cell phone.

"Yay! Yara's coming home with Daddy!"

I can't believe Ronny calls my father "daddy." I scowl. "That was suspiciously fast, don't you think?"

"What?" Mari asks.

"We *just* put up the flyers. Someone already found her?" I wonder if the same person "found" the other three missing dogs.

"Lucky for us." Mari smiles.

"Lucky for them, they'll get a fat reward."

Mari puts her hands on her skinny hips. "Don't be so cynical."

"What's *cynical?*" Crispy asks.

"Distrustful," I say. Okay, I admit it. I read the dictionary for fun. I'm up to the letter *J.* Mrs. Cheever, my English teacher, says I have to work on my vocabulary if I want to be a standout journalist. "I'm not cynical. But a good detective has to be suspicious in order to find her suspects."

"Fine, Sherlock. You can exercise your brain. We're going to celebrate." Mari throws her hands in the air. "Who wants popcorn and gummy bears?"

"For dinner?" Crispy looks at me. At home, Mom never lets us eat "junk food."

"What if this person didn't *find* Yara but already had her?" I stand up for emphasis. "What if they're kidnapping dogs so they can collect the rewards?"

2
THE HOLE IN THE WALL

THE NEXT MORNING, MRS. PATEL USES TONGS to hand us each a white square of yumminess called *badam barfi*. It sounds funny, but *Barf* means "snow" in three languages: Hindi, Urdu, and Persian. *Barfi* is my new favorite dessert. It's made out of cashews, milk, and sugar. The aroma of delicious Indian desserts is just one reason I love the bakery. I always feel happier seeing the brightly colored sweets in the display case.

Good thing Mom doesn't know how many treats we eat when we're helping Mrs. Patel at the bakery, which is in downtown Lemontree Heights, a five-minute drive from our farm. I pop the barfi into my mouth and head through the kitchen to the back. Crispy and Butler tag behind.

I hope I get another case soon. Without classes, I'm bored. I guess I'm weird, because I already miss school and we've only been out for a week. Summer vacation always feels like waiting around for something to happen. At least it used to before we set up the pet detective service at Patel Pastries. Crispy and Butler are helping me clean out the storage closet and arrange our office.

I wipe my sticky fingers on my jeans and open the door to the closet—or I should say, our office.

"Hey, Carrot, I made something for you," Butler says with a smile. Butler is in my honors English class. I don't know why, but he follows me around like a puppy.

"Don't call me *Carrot*!" I hate it when people call me *carrottop*. I don't call people with brown hair *Brownie*.

He pulls a wooden sign from a shopping bag.

The sign has *Kassy O'Roarke, Pet Detective* burnt into the wood.

Hot buttered cheese grits! My own sign. This really makes the business look professional.

Butler blushes as he holds it out to me. "See, I attached a leather cord on the back so we can hang it on the door." He points to it. "I can hang it for you."

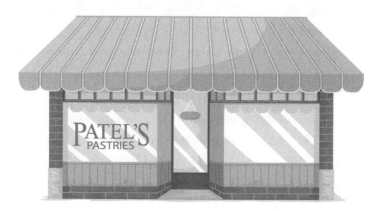

"Thanks."

He pulls a small hammer and a nail from out of his back pants pocket. *Wow! He comes prepared.* I hand the sign back to him. *So cool.*

While Butler is hammering, I glance around. Inside, the closet is still a mess. Old paint cans are stacked along one wall. The shelves are covered in cobwebs. A pile of dusty, faded magazines and newspapers almost reaches the ceiling. So does a stack of dilapidated cardboard boxes filled with who knows what.

In the corner of the doorframe, a fat spider dangles from its web—right above my head. I point to it to warn Crispy.

"I hate spiders," he says as he scurries into the tiny room. Freddie squeaks in protest. He loves spiders and thinks they make tasty treats. I guess we all have our phobias. Mine is bats.

"Where did all this stuff come from?" Crispy asks.

"Good question." I kick a rusty wooden-handled tool out of my way.

Butler leans against the doorframe. "Originally this building was a saddle-making shop."

"How do you know?" I turn over a five-gallon plastic bucket and use it as a stool.

"The owner told my mom." Butler takes a seat on a stack of boxes. "Over the years, it has been a pharmacy, a paper store, and now a bakery."

Crispy is digging around in a dusty old pile of stuff. "Look at this!" He holds up a raggedy magazine. *Agricultural Museum.* He opens the cover and reads from inside, "On the Culture of Potatoes by Bath Papers."

"What kind of name is Bath Papers?" Butler asks.

"What kind of potatoes have culture?" I chime in.

Crispy blinks at me and then continues flipping through the pages. "There's an article on how to make paper out of vegetables."

"Is it also by Mr. —or Ms.—Papers?" I reach over and take the magazine. *Brussels sprouts!* "This is over two hundred years old. The date is August 29, 1810."

"What else is in that stack?" Butler joins Crispy in riffling through the crumbling magazines and newspapers.

A scratching noise from the corner startles me. I twist around and spot Freddie's furry tail disappearing into the wall. I glance over at Crispy, who is busy rifling through the musty old papers. I have to get the ferret back out of the hole in the wall before my brother notices he's gone and has a conniption. *Conniption* is one of my dictionary words. Mom had a conniption when our cougar cub, Apollo, went missing a few weeks ago. Luckily, using my journalism and detective skills, I got him back.

I crawl on my hands and knees over more strange antique tools and weird pieces of wood until I reach the hole in the wall. "Freddie," I whisper. "Come back here." The hole is only about the size of a tangerine, but ferrets are remarkably dexterous and can squeeze through the smallest holes . . . so can mice, rats, and bats. I shudder. *What else might be in there with Freddie?* I lean down and try to peek into the hole. I can smell him, but I can't see him. I grit my teeth and stick my index finger through the opening. *Chicken-fried steak!* Something sharp bites my finger. When I yank my hand away, I knock over a hat stand.

Drat. The crash gets Crispy's attention. "Where's Freddie?"

"Inside the wall." I plop down and sit cross-legged, holding my scratched finger.

"What?" Crispy cries as Butler says, "You're hurt."

Butler takes a handkerchief from the pocket of his khaki pants. I thought only old ladies and old-school movie heroes carried hankies.

"I got bit by a rat . . . or something." I suck on my stinging finger.

"What if it has rabies?"

"Thanks a lot, Butt-ler."

"Freddie! Freddie!" Crispy is beside himself, searching every corner of the closet. "How will we find him in all this junk?"

"I told you, he's in the wall."

Crispy's mouth gapes open like a beached catfish.

"With the rabid rat," I tease.

"That's not funny." Crispy drops to his knees next to the wall and lies down, staring into the hole. "Freddie. Here, boy."

"Ferrets aren't dogs. They don't come—"

"Freddie does. I trained him."

I put my hand on Crispy's shoulder. "Listen."

"What's that noise?" Butler asks, joining us in the corner.

There's lots of rustling and a weird clinking. *What is Freddie doing in there? And who is in there with him? Or what?*

"What if he's hurt?" Crispy whines.

"He's fine. He's probably having the time of his life." I stand up and knock on the wall. It sounds hollow.

"You're the pet detective. Can't you get him out?" Crispy is trying to shove his hand through the hole, but even with his small hand, he can only get two fingers in.

I pat the pocket of my spy vest. Good thing I replenished my emergency granola bar supply. "We'll have to lure him out."

A knock on the office door makes me jump. Mrs. Patel sticks her head in. "Everything okay?" she asks. Luckily, she doesn't see the hole.

"All good," Butler says.

I nod in agreement.

Crispy is on the verge of tears.

"Is Percy alright?"

"He's fine," I fib.

Mrs. Patel looks doubtful. "Can someone help me up front? I have a cake due to come out of the oven and there's a customer." Mrs. P. has a smudge of flour across her round cheek. She wipes her hands on her apron. "Just for a few minutes."

"Sure." I give Butler a pleading look and hand him the granola bar. "Freddie loves these almost as much as dog biscuits."

I follow Mrs. Patel back out into the bakery. I like her. She's teaching me how to bake delicious desserts. Mrs. Patel is always laughing and happy. And on special occasions, she wears beautiful silky draped dresses called *saris*. All Mom does on special occasions is change out of her overalls into scrubs.

Mrs. Patel drags the back of her hand across her forehead. "Warm in here." She heads through the swinging door into the kitchen. I keep going around the corner into the storefront.

The storefront has a glass display case full of treats, and a cash register, which I've learned to operate. There are two small tile-topped café tables each with bright green metal chairs. A lanky teenage boy jumps up from one of the tables when he sees me. His black leather jacket and army boots make him look tough in a cool sort of way. He flashes a crooked smile. I'm guessing he must be fourteen . . . older than me, but younger than Butler's brother, Oliver.

"Got any doughnuts?" When he gets up from the table, his shaggy blond hair flops over one eye, and he tries to shake it out of the way.

"We've got *gulab jamun*." I point inside the display case. "They're Indian doughnuts soaked in syrup."

"'Indian' like Native American?" He leans against the case.

"No, 'Indian' as in *India*. South Asia." I scowl. I don't like him getting fingerprints on the glass. "They're good. Want to try one?" Mrs. Patel always gives out free samples. She knows once folks taste her desserts, they'll be hooked.

"Sure." He holds out his hand.

I open the case, grab the tongs, drop a doughnut ball into a cupcake paper, and hand it across the counter to him.

"What's your name?" He bites into the doughnut. "Aren't you kinda young to work here?" he asks with his mouth full.

"I'm Kassandra O'Roarke." My friends call me Kassy, but this dude is not my friend. "I'm almost thirteen. And I'm just helping out."

"I'm James, but everyone calls me Slug." He extends a sticky hand. "I'm almost fifteen."

"Do you live in Lemontree Heights?" I've never seen him before. He must be new.

"I'm like a bird. I don't live anywhere."

"Even birds have nests, except for penguins." On my tip-toes, I reach over the counter and wipe the glass with a rag. "What about your parents?" I cringe thinking about my own parents. Dad is always saying "earth to Kassy." I still wish he'd just come back home.

"I'm an orphan. I don't have parents." Slug licks his fingers. "Pretty good doughnut."

"Not even foster parents or a guardian?"

"I don't want to talk about my foster parents." He shoves his hands into his pockets.

"You're like a cuckoo chick." I take the opportunity to wipe off the rest of his fingerprints. "Cuckoos lay their eggs in another bird's nest to raise."

"How do you know so much about birds?"

"My mom is a vet. She taught me everything about animals."

"Why are you wearing a fishing vest?" Slug leans against the counter again.

I'm about to tell him I'm a pet detective when a ruckus makes me turn around.

Crispy runs into the storefront, yelling. "Come quick. Freddie is hurt."

"Who is Freddie?" Slug asks.

"My brother's stinky ferret." I drop the rag into the sink behind the counter. "I've got to go." I put my hand on Crispy's shoulder. "Come on. Let's help Freddie." I head back to the closet. If Slug wants any more desserts, he'll just have to wait.

As I run into the closet, I hear Freddie squeaking. My heart leaps into my throat. *Shrimp and grits! What am I going to do?* Except for the tiny hole near the floor, the wall is solid.

"Did you try luring him out with the granola bar?" I ask.

Crispy nods. Tears roll down his cheeks. "Butler went home to get a saw." Even his voice is soggy.

Butler lives half a mile away. Even on his bicycle, he won't be back for at least ten minutes.

Down on all fours, I pick up a corner of the granola bar and stick it through the hole. "Come on, Freddie." The squeaking is getting louder, and now it is accompanied by a jingling. *What's going on inside this wall?* I wiggle the bar around. *Come on, Freddie! Your best friend is out here having kittens.*

"He's hurt!" Crispy yowls. "The rabid rat's got him."

"He could take on a rat." I hope I'm right for Crispy's sake.

When the squealing turns to shrieking, I start to panic.

3
THE KEY

"THE FERRET IS INSIDE THAT WALL?" A voice comes from behind me.

Chicken-fried steak. Slug followed me. Before I ask him what he's doing here, he starts kicking at the wall with his big booted foot.

"Don't do that!" I yank on the sleeve of his leather jacket.

Slug whacks the wall again with his boot, and the little hole turns into a big one.

Holy cannoli! The building owner isn't going to be happy. And if Mrs. Patel evicts me, I won't have an office.

As the chalky dust settles, Freddie scampers out holding a key in his mouth.

"Freddie!" Crispy lunges at the ferret and scoops him up. "You're okay." They nuzzle each other like two reunited littermates.

"What's this?" I take the key away from Freddie.

"It's a key," Slug says.

"Thank you, Captain Obvious." I examine the key. It's rusty and heavy.

"Captain Obvious, I'm Percy." My brother grins over at the new boy.

I roll my eyes. "This is Slug. He's a new bird in town."

"Slug?" My brother giggles. "Like a gastropod?"

When Slug narrows his eyes and holds up a fist, my brother stops laughing. "*Slug* as in *slugger*."

"This key is really old." I turn it over in my hand. "Look at the design on the top." I hold the key up to the light. The top of the key forms two interlocking letters, *L* and *J*. I glance down at the hole. "What else is behind that wall?"

Before I can stop him, Slug kicks another chunk out.

"Stop kicking the wall in!" I bend down and inspect the mess. Chalky chunks of wall and white powder cover the floor under the hole. The musty smell of centuries of mold and mildew waft out of the opening. Not a great smell for a bakery.

Shhh! I put my finger to my lips. With all the ruckus, I'm surprised Mrs. Patel hasn't come back to see what's going on. I hear voices out front. She must have customers. We'd better clean up this mess before she sees it.

I lean over and peek inside the hole. *Chicken-fried steak!* Just on the other side, a small metal box lays open. I stick my hand in and snatch it from the jaws of the hole.

There's a key-shaped wooden frame built into the box. I set the key inside, and it fits perfectly. *Wow! What a cool treasure.* I slide the box into one of my vest pockets, then lean over so my head is almost touching the dirty floor. *Disgusting.* Past the pile of rubble, about six inches deeper into the hole and behind a veil of dusty cobwebs, there's another wall made of bricks.

"Be careful!" Crispy shouts. "The rabid rat, remember."

I glance back at my brother, then extend my arm inside the hole. "Ahhhh!" I scream and yank my hand back.

"Did it bite you again?" Crispy lifts Freddie, and the ferret curls around his neck. "I'll get the first aid kit."

"Gotcha!" I laugh. "Just joking." I wave my hand around.

"Very funny." When Slug laughs it sounds like he's snorting water up his nose.

I take a deep breath and plunge my arm back into the hole. *We've already found a box and a key. Who knows what else is in there?* I lean further in and feel something hard. I claw at it with my fingertips. It moves an inch. I claw again. It moves another inch. I almost have my fingertips around its corner when it slips out of my grasp.

"What's in there?" Slug asks.

I clamber to my hands and knees and block the hole before Slug can interfere. I hold my breath and stick my whole head inside. *Bad idea.* Spiderwebs brush against my face. I tighten my lips. Squinting, I peer into the tiny alley between the walls. Slowly, I reach my hand into the dark maw. I feel cobwebs, dust, and what I'm guessing are insect carcasses. *Gross!* I wrinkle my nose. The smell has gone from dank to foul.

The tips of my fingers touch the hard corner again. I turn my head sideways and lean my shoulder into the hole so I can stretch my arm a bit further. With the tips of my fingers, I grasp at the hard object again, dragging it a little closer. I claw at it with my fingernail, and it moves a millimeter closer. Finally, I get my hand around the end of it and slide it into the space between the two walls. Sitting back on my haunches, I grab the thing with both hands and pull it out into the light. *Jackpot!* An engraved wooden box covered in dirt.

"What is it?" Crispy asks, coming over to my side.

I glance up into two beady sets of eager eyes, my brother's and the ferret's. Gently, I open the wooden box. "It's a book!" A leather-bound book tied shut with a leather cord. I remove the book, unwrap the cord, and open the cover.

"An old book." Slug grabs the book out of my hands.

"No! It's fragile." I beg him to give it back.

Freddie jumps from my brother's shoulders onto the top of Slug's mop of hair. When the ferret reaches down and bites Slug's nose, he drops the book. It's like the critter understood me.

As Slug curses and rubs his nose, I snatch the book up off the floor and hug it to my chest. "The key and the book may be clues to some ancient mystery."

"Or maybe a treasure map and the key to a treasure chest," Crispy chimes in.

"Little kids with big imaginations!" Slug scoffs.

"Who are you calling little?" Crispy puffs out his chest. "I'm eight."

"Okay, tough guy." Slug chuckles. "Chill out." He looks over my shoulder. "Aren't you going to read it?"

"Of course I am." I was actually hoping to read it in the privacy of my own room back at home. I've got to get rid of Slug. I don't want to share the book's secrets with some punk I just met. I clutch the book tighter.

"Let me read it," Slug says. "I'm the oldest."

"Not true." Crispy scratches the ferret's head. "Freddie is two years old, which is thirty-two in human years."

"But can he read?" Slug lunges at me.

I jump backward and topple a stack of boxes. As I tumble to the floor, the book flies out of my hands. "Get the book," I shout at my brother.

Crispy sprints toward the book, but with one leap, Slug gets to it first. He grabs it and rips it open.

"Be careful," I yell. "You'll tear it."

"Hush, girlie." Slug grins down at me. He reads from the inside page of the book, "This is the diary of Lyncoya Jackson." He looks up with wide eyes. "The first entry is dated July 28, 1827."

"It's over one hundred and ninety years old." I scramble to my feet.

He tucks the book under his arm and takes out his cell phone. "Lyncoya Jackson," he repeats. "Wowsers. You won't believe this!" He snorts. "'Born in 1811, Lyncoya Jackson was an orphaned Creek Native American. American president Andrew Jackson sent Lyncoya to his home outside of Nashville, the Hermitage, to be raised as his own in 1813.'"

"President Andrew Jackson." *Whew.* I whistle.

"He was an orphan," Crispy says.

"Just like you," I say to Slug.

"This must be worth something." Slug rewraps the leather cord around the book and stuffs it inside his shirt. "I can sell it."

"No! It's mine." I pounce.

"Freddie found it," Crispy says. "Finders keepers."

"Possession is nine-tenths of the law." Slug steps around a pile of newspapers and makes for the door.

Tears sprout from my eyes. I know detectives, spies, and journalists don't cry, but I can't help it. I have to protect the book and discover its secrets. Its history is worth a whole lot more than money.

Mrs. Patel appears in the doorway. "What's happened? Kassy, honey, are you all right?"

"Slug took my book!" I point at the thief.

She narrows her eyes. "Please return Kassandra's book."

"But it's my—"

She stands with her hands on her wide hips blocking the doorway. The streaks of flour across her face look like war paint. "Return the book, young man, and then go home to your parents."

"He's an orphan," Crispy pipes up.

Mrs. Patel gives my brother the side-eye, then turns to Slug. "You're the Harrison boy, aren't you? Son of Johnny Harrison? Your parents just moved into—"

Slug's cell phone ringtone is some loud rock song. He holds up one hand and then answers his phone. "Okay, Mom." He nods his head as if his mom can see him. He shifts from foot to foot. "I'm on my way." He flashes a sheepish smile as he stuffs his phone back in his jeans pocket. "I've got to go."

Mrs. Patel holds out her hand and wiggles her fingers. "Kassandra's book, please, Mr. Harrison."

Slug scowls, removes the book from his shirt, and hands it to Mrs. Patel.

She steps out of the doorway and lets him by.

He turns back and smiles sweetly at me. "I'll be back tomorrow afternoon, and I'd love to help you solve the mysteries of that book."

"Kassy's a detective," Crispy says. "She doesn't need your help, right, Freddie?" He kisses the ferret's little black nose. Sometimes my brother is so sincere it hurts.

"It's so deadly boring out here in the suburbs." He lowers his head and gives me a pleading look. When his blond hair flops over one eye, he looks like a heartthrob from a boy band, the kind my cheerleader nemesis, Kelly Finkelman, is always cooing about. "Please. I just want to come along for the adventure."

"Okay," I say in a moment of weakness. "See you tomorrow."

"What happened to the wall?" Mrs. Patel wipes her hands on her apron and heads for the hole. "I've had customers and then a big delivery. And you're back here wrecking the place?"

"Freddie was stuck, and Slug kicked the wall in." Crispy snuggles the ferret. "Right, Freddie?"

"We'll work extra hours in the bakery to pay to have it fixed." With my foot, I sweep pieces of rubble back into the hole.

"It doesn't matter." When Mrs. Patel sighs, she seems to shrink a couple of inches, and she's already short. "Holes in the wall . . . animals in the closet . . . The bakery won't be around much longer. What else could go wrong?"

"What?" I freeze. "Why not?"

"The bakery is just not taking off like I'd hoped. I'm not making enough to pay the rent." She brushes loose hairs back into her messy bun. "If I can't come up with the rent money by the end of the month, I'll have to close."

"No." I stomp my foot. "That's not fair!"

"As they say, all is fair in love and business." Mrs. Patel gives me a weak smile. "You kids don't worry. It'll be okay. But maybe you can be more careful about the wall and leave the ferret at home?"

A bell rings, signaling someone coming through the front door. "I'd better go. We have a customer." Mrs. Patel shuffles around the junk and out the door.

As she goes out, Butler comes in, holding a saw. "You rescued Freddie?"

Freddie chirps and toots in answer.

"I hope your mom's not going to give away more samples for free." I pick up chunks of wall and drop them into a trash bag. "She's got to start charging—"

Crispy interrupts. "Apollo says it's not what you have—"

"Not what you have but what you give away that matters. I know." I wipe my dusty palms on my jeans. "But Apollo is a cougar cub and not a businesswoman."

Freddie jumps down off Crispy's shoulders and darts past me toward the hole. "No, you don't!" I scoop him up. "Phew. You stink!" I hand the wriggling furball back to my brother. "Don't let him out of your sight."

"Maybe there's more treasure and stuff inside the wall." Crispy plops down on top of a wooden crate.

"Treasure?" Butler asks.

"What are we going to do?" I hop up off the floor and sit on a stack of boxes. "We've got to save the bakery."

"How?" Crispy is scratching his stinky ferret under the chin.

"I don't know." Distracted by the Patel Pastries conundrum, I absentmindedly untie the leather cord and flip through the diary. One page is full of numbers, another has a pocket with a thick paper triangle tucked into it, and another has lines and symbols. I turn the book around and stare at the page. "Crispy, you're right! It *is* a treasure map."

4
THE FIRST RIDDLE

THE NEXT DAY, I GET UP EARLY to do my chores. Slopping Poseidon the pig, throwing bananas to Chewbacca the chimp, tossing feed to Kylo Ren the rooster, emptying the compost bucket of veggie peelings into Raider the raccoon's dish, and setting a block of ant protein in front of Athena the anteater, I keep thinking, *if only we could find the treasure, we could save the bakery.*

I'm on autopilot as I leave the barn to shovel manure out of Morpheus the pony's corral. By the time I get to Spittoon the camel's enclosure, I've hatched a plan. I pat Spittoon on his soft, fuzzy muzzle. "Good boy." The camel nudges my arm with his slobbery lips and then sneezes. *Yuck!* I wipe my slimy forearm off on my overalls, then fling a big handful of hay over the fence.

Spittoon's best friend is Apollo the cougar cub, but the camel is allergic to cats. Mom says we're always allergic to what we love most, and with love comes danger. Maybe she's right. I love adventure and mystery. And while they don't make me sneeze, they sure can be dangerous.

The image of dogcatcher Pinkerton Killjoy with his bushy mustache flashes into my mind. *Ha.* Squirting Elmer's glue at his ugly mug got me grounded for a month. Luckily, Mom is so busy with the vet clinic and the petting zoo that she forgets I'm grounded. As long as I do my chores, she's happy.

As I round the corner with the wheelbarrow full of manure, the wind shifts and the breeze blows the pungent smell of fresh pony poo. I dump the mother lode behind the barn, then zip back inside to collect the morning offerings from the other animals. By the time I'm done, I smell like a dung heap. The sun is already getting hot, and the heat intensifies all the animal odors. Actually, the familiar scents of muddy pig and dusty chimp are reassuring.

After the recent incident with Apollo, I always double-check every enclosure at the conclusion of my morning chores. Crispy joins me as I make one more trip through the petting zoo and I'll be done. Then I can get back to the mystery of the diary and the rusty key. As I whiz past each cage to make sure its inhabitant is fed and happy, a cacophony of hoots, squeals, purrs, and chirps echoes through the huge barn.

Apollo, check. He's playing with one of Darth Vader's tail feathers that drifted into the pen. *Raider, check.* He's dipping his paws into his water dish and then washing his face. *Athena, check.* She's licking her ant block, her long snout sucking up insects like a funnel.

"Did you know Athena is in the suborder *Vermilingua*? It means 'worm tongue.'"

"Worm tongue." Crispy thinks that's hilarious.

Chewbacca, check. She's huddled in the corner of her enclosure. *Wait a second! What is she cradling in her arms? Brussels sprouts!* The chimp is holding a gray tabby kitten. *Where did it come from?* I open the gate, enter the cage, and stare down at the purring bundle. "What are you doing with a cat?"

The chimp just looks up at me with determination in her black eyes. When I reach out for the tabby kitten, Chewbacca swirls around to face the back corner of her pen. She won't let me near the cat. I notice the kitten has a pink collar, but Chewy won't let me look at it. *Sigh.* I have to report this to Mom.

Mom is in her clinic, which is attached to our house. It used to be the garage. She doesn't like it when I interrupt her at work unless it's an emergency. I don't know if a cat in the

petting zoo counts, but it *is* a breach of security. *I mean, how did a cat get into the barn?* The doors were shut and locked . . . unless Crispy left the door open again.

I wait in the clinic, watching dogs and cats being dragged into exam rooms. Nobody is happy about a trip to the vet. For something to do, I hand out dog bones to nervous canines.

Between patients, Mom comes out to the waiting room and asks, "What's up?"

I tell her about the cat in the chimp's pen.

"You didn't leave the door open last night, did you?"

I can't believe Mom thinks I'd be that irresponsible. I tighten my lips and shake my head.

"Always something," she says. Then she returns to her furry patients. "At lunchtime, I'll go investigate."

I don't need to check my spy watch—the growling in my stomach tells me it must be close to lunchtime. I decide to wait for Mom here. I curl up on the end of a bench in the waiting room and nibble on one of my emergency granola bars while looking through the diary. I study a drawing with tiny squares and triangles, trying to figure out if it's a map. Turning it around doesn't help. Maybe it's in code. I'm concentrating so hard that I don't hear Mom until she's standing right over me.

"Show me the cat." Mom heads for the door.

Mom and I go to the barn to investigate. Sure enough, the cat is still there. Chewbacca and the tabby kitten are cuddled up, sleeping. Mom snaps a couple of pictures with her cell phone.

"I'll post these on the neighborhood list and in the clinic." With her pixie haircut and petite horse-print scrubs, she looks more like a kid than a doctor. "I've got to get back to work."

Mom ruffles my hair. "Bring the cat some kibble from the clinic. And make some peanut butter sandwiches for you and your brother. There's some chocolate zucchini cake left."

Vegetables for dessert. No thanks. Mom's gluten-free, vegetable-laden desserts leave something to be desired, especially after tasting Mrs. Patel's delicious sugary treats.

"Keep an eye on your brother. And don't leave the yard." I follow Mom back to the clinic. "We'll figure out what to do with the cat after I'm finished working."

Since Dad left, Mom has had to do everything. No wonder she has purple bags under her eyes. Maybe if I find the treasure, she won't have to work so hard.

Back in the clinic, Mom goes to the back to print out a flyer for the Found Pets bulletin board.

The clinic smells of bleach and wet dog. A puppy on a leash sniffs at my shoe, and his little tail whacks my leg.

"Hello, little guy." When I bend down to pet him, he makes a puddle on the floor.

"Oh no. So sorry." The puppy's person puts her hand over her mouth. She's trying not to laugh. Her blue fingernails flutter in front of her face.

A tech swoops in with paper towels and disinfectant spray. Mom is right behind her but doesn't even notice. Puppy accidents are a daily occurrence.

I follow Mom over to the bulletin board.

"Are there always so many lost pets?" The corkboard for Lost Pets is completely covered with flyers offering rewards. I should try to help these people get their furry friends back. After all, I am a pet detective.

"We've had a flurry of lost pets lately. Maybe someone has lost this little gal." Mom pushes a pin through the flyer with the picture of Chewbacca's cat friend. "When I have time, I'll see if she has a chip."

"She was wearing a pink collar, so she must belong to somebody. Cats aren't usually born with collars in the wild. Sometimes, but not often."

Mom smiles. "Cute. Go make some lunch for you and your brother. I'll be done in a couple of hours." Mom's sneakers squeak as she crosses the polished linoleum floor. "There are kale chips in the pantry."

As if that's going to happen. Even Crispy draws the line at kale chips.

One of the lost pet flyers catches my attention. The tabby cat in the picture looks a lot like Chewbacca's new feline friend. I jot down the phone number in my spy notebook. *Should I call now or wait until Mom gets off work?* I decide I'd better wait. Mom is not always so keen on me taking matters into my own hands. She tells me to think before acting. Meanwhile, Dad tells me I overthink everything and need to just do it. Parents can be so confusing. I rip the flyer down, fold it, and stuff it into my pocket.

After lunch, I retreat upstairs to my bedroom to read the diary. Crispy follows me and stands outside my door singing "Let It Go" until I can't take it anymore and let him in.

"What does it say?" he asks, plopping down on my bed. He and Freddie both stare down at me.

I'm sitting on the floor, leaning up against the bed, carefully looking through the diary. "Lyncoya Jackson was sixteen when he wrote this. He apprenticed in the bakery's building back when it was a saddle shop." I turn the page. "I think he hid some gold."

"Gold!" Crispy bounces up and down on my bed like a kangaroo. Jostled around like a potato on a trampoline, Freddie toots in protest.

"Listen to this." I read from the diary: "'My mother gave me the gold . . .' Hmm. I can't read the next words. But then it says, '. . . in case something happens to me, I'm making a map so this treasure is not lost forever.'"

"Wow!" Crispy gives Freddie belly rubs. "How much do you think the treasure is worth?"

"I don't know. But if we find the gold, we can save the bakery."

"I thought you were a pet detective, not a gold detective." Crispy kneels on the bed with his hands bent in front of his chest and his tongue out like a panting dog. Freddie crawls up his arm and onto his head.

Why did I ever let these goofballs into my bedroom? "A detective follows clues. The puzzles, symbols, and numbers in this diary are clues."

"What kind of clues?"

"Like your riddles." Crispy loves riddles. He recently made up a bunch for me—that was part of my last case.

"I love riddles!"

Like I didn't know that. I continue flipping through the pages and stop on a list of three riddles. "Here's a whole page for you." I hand the book to my brother. "What do you make of these?"

He narrows his brows in concentration. "They're hard."

I take the diary back and read the first one out loud: "'Marking a life lost, when firmly in place. An enduring epitaph, inscribed on my face.'"

"What does it mean?" Crispy hops off the bed and joins me on the floor.

"*A life lost,*" I repeat. "Must be death." I stare down at the riddle. "*Inscribed on my face* . . . something written on a face. Face of what?"

"A clock?" Crispy suggests.

I rack my brain for other types of faces. "What has a face besides a clock?"

Crispy counts on his fingers. "Animals, people, coins, arguments, nails—"

"Nails have heads, not faces. How do arguments have faces?"

"Dad says not to take everything at face value."

I shake my head. "Okay." Sometimes I think my brother is a few cards short of a full deck.

A knock at the door startles me. Before I can say "enter," Mom opens the door.

"What's that?" She points at the book.

Holy hijack! I hope she's not going to take it away or make me put it back.

"We found it in the wall at the bakery," Crispy pipes up. "It's a treasure map."

"It looks old." Mom holds out her hand, and I give her the diary. I hold my breath, waiting for her to give it back.

"It's an old treasure map. Kassy's going to find the treasure and save the bakery." Crispy grins. Boy, he can't keep anything on the down low. *What a blabbermouth.*

"That's nice," Mom says, handing the diary back to me. "Now, let's find the owners of Chewbacca's kitten friend."

Whew. I thought she was going to continue the third degree about the diary. Luckily, she's so busy with her clinic and the petting zoo that she doesn't have time to pry. I pull the flyer from my pocket and unfold it. "Is this the same cat?" I show Mom.

"Gray tabby with a pink collar, just like Chewy's friend." Mom smiles. "I think we've hit the jackpot!" She pulls out her cell phone and dials the number from the flyer. After a minute of chatting, she nods her head.

I hold my breath.

Mom slips her phone back into the pocket of her scrubs. "We have a winner!"

Crispy does a fist pump, and I give him a high five. Then I have an idea.

"I should find all those missing pets and collect the rewards to use to help Mrs. Patel."

"Mrs. Patel needs help?" Mom looks up from her phone.

"She doesn't have enough money to pay the rent."

"But the bakery just opened."

"She gives away too many treats. But if I find the missing pets and collect the rewards—"

Crispy frowns. "Apollo says we shouldn't profit from the misery of others."

I give him the side-eye. He's talking to the animals again . . . and they're talking back. "Apollo is full of words of wisdom," I say, my voice dripping with sarcasm.

"Apollo says he's the conscience of this outfit."

Mom and I burst out laughing. Crispy looks hurt.

"Apollo is right," Mom says, trying to stop laughing. "He's pretty smart for a cougar cub."

"Show Mom the riddle." Crispy points under my bed where I've hidden the diary. "I bet she can solve it."

I scowl at him. I can solve it without Mom's help, and I don't want her to get any ideas about taking away the diary. "An enduring epitaph inscribed on my face." I repeat the second half of the riddle by heart. Even though I've passed *E* in the dictionary, I can't remember what *epitaph* means.

"Is that part of your scavenger hunt?" Mom smiles. "Won't it be cheating if I help you?"

"No!" Crispy and I say in unison.

"Enduring epitaph . . ." Mom scratches her head. "An inscription in memory of someone." Her eyes light up. "How about—"

"Headstone!" I interrupt.

"Headstone?" Crispy asks.

"You know, grave marker, tombstone." I clap my hands together. "That's it!" I'm one step closer to the treasure. *But which tombstone?*

5

HAIRY PAWTER

IN THE SUMMER, THE DAYS BLEND TOGETHER. Mom works every day but Sunday. And the petting zoo is open daily during the summer. Mom had to hire extra staff to sell tickets and show folks around. Crispy and I feed the animals and clean their cages before the zoo opens and then again after it closes. I like hanging out in the barn, but only when the petting zoo is closed and no one is around. With all the kids coming in, especially on weekends, it's too noisy and crowded for me.

Judging by the line outside the barn door, it must be Saturday, the busiest day at the zoo. The sun is brutal, and sweaty, red-faced kids hold their parents' hands, waiting to meet Apollo and the gang. Crispy is going up and down the line offering ice-cold lemonade. Mom promised that if we help out at the zoo this morning, we can go to the library this afternoon. She only works half-days on Saturday, and, luckily for us, she hired Toby Brown to run the petting zoo during business hours. Toby was born with one leg shorter than the other, and he always looks like he's dancing.

I'm itching to get back to the bakery and look for more clues in the wall, but first I want to do a little research on Lyncoya Jackson. If we do find more treasures in the wall, then I'll know what I'm looking at. Tomorrow, Crispy and I are scheduled to help Mrs. Patel at the bakery. Maybe after we're finished, Butler's older brother, Oliver, will drive us to the cemetery to check out tombstones. I don't even want to ask Mom to take us to the cemetery.

I squeeze past the bottleneck of visitors at the zoo entrance and patrol the barn. It's really more like a huge warehouse with a twenty-foot ceiling. Giant fans at either end of the building create a vortex of cool air. Only open for five minutes and already the place is packed with kids wanting to pet Chewbacca, Poseidon, and Athena. Outside, folks are feeding carrots to Morpheus and Spittoon.

I pace back and forth, kicking hay across the concrete floor and hoping lunchtime comes soon. I'm eager to get back to the treasure hunt.

"Can we pet the monkey?" a little girl asks, pulling on my pant leg. She points at Chewbacca, who is sitting in the corner of her pen chewing on something. We don't call her Chewy for nothing!

"Let's give her a banana." I lead the girl and her mom to Chewy's enclosure. I grab a miniature banana from a bowl outside the cage and hand it to the little girl. She glances up at her mom, then bites the banana herself.

"Honey, we need to peel it first," her mom says.

"Chewbacca likes them with the peelings on." I point to the chimp. "The banana is for her."

The little girl scowls at me.

"Here." I open a small window in the gate to Chewy's pen. "Hold the banana out and she'll come over to say hello."

The girl puts her finger in her mouth and looks up at her mom again. Her mom nods. The girl sticks her tiny hand into the window and drops the banana inside Chewy's pen.

Usually, Chewy drops everything for a banana, especially the mini bananas. But today, she refuses to budge. She's too busy chewing on what looks like a diamond-studded baby blue leather strap. *What has she got ahold of now?*

"You wait here," I say to the girl and her mom. "I'll go get her." When I open the gate and climb into Chewy's enclosure, a crowd forms around the pen. Suddenly, I'm the most interesting animal in the petting zoo.

"What have you got there?" I offer Chewy the mini banana as a trade, but she just gives me the stink eye, as if to say, 'Don't you dare take my new toy.'

I wave the banana in front of her face, and she follows it with her eyes. I can tell she's tempted. When I peel the banana and pretend to take a bite, she drops the leather strap and snatches the banana out of my hand. The crowd erupts in applause. I bend down and pick up the strap while she gobbles up her treat. They must think I'm taking a bow, because they start clapping again.

The strap turns out to be a collar with diamond studs, about ten inches long with a small silver buckle on the end and a dog tag attached. The dog's name is etched on the tag: HAIRY PAWTER. *Ha ha!*

"Where'd you get this?" I ask the chimp.

She just shrugs.

Why does Chewbacca have a dog collar? First a feline friend and now a dog collar. *What's going on?* I stuff the collar into a vest pocket and climb back out of the pen. The crowd gathers around me like I'm some sort of celebrity. The kids are asking questions and pulling on my vest. I throw them a couple granola bars and make a beeline for the barn door.

Outside, I find Crispy showing off, riding Spittoon backward while balancing Freddie on his head. He's turned the petting zoo into a three-ring circus. When Freddie jumps onto the camel's head, the kids roar with laughter. Yeah, my brother and his farting ferret are regular clowns.

I wave to Crispy. He waves back, slides off the camel's back, and then catches Freddie in his arms, to the crowd's delight. I shake my head. *What a ham!*

I check my spy watch. *Drat!* It's stopped. I tap it. Nothing. *Sigh.* I guess it needs a new battery. It's a pretty cool watch—when it works. It has a compass and a voice disguiser, which I haven't used yet.

Judging by the sun's position in the sky—straight overhead—it must be about noon. If Mom would let me have a cell phone, I'd know what time it is. I could even search the Internet to learn more about Andrew Jackson's adopted son, Lyncoya. As it is, I'll have to wait until Mom takes us to the public library and use their computers.

Mom only lets us use her computer to do our homework, and she watches us like a hawk. No surfing allowed. She says there's plenty to do in the real world without burying your head in the virtual world. She says fresh air and chicken poop are better for us than Instagram and video games. So, no Internet until we get to the library.

In the meantime, I'm going to learn everything I can from the diary and hope we find more clues in the wall of the storage closet . . . I mean *my detective office*. I skip inside the house to make lunch. If I have the peanut butter sandwiches ready when Mom gets done in the clinic, then we can eat right away and get to the library sooner.

Our kitchen looks like a science lab. Mom always has a weird collection of mason jars growing fungus or bacteria or other disgusting stuff strewn across the kitchen counters. I stand at the far corner of the counter, as far away from Mom's creepy experiments as possible. Slathering big blobs of peanut butter and strawberry jam on Mom's store-bought gluten-free bread so it doesn't taste so much like cardboard, I rehearse the speech I'll use to get Oliver to drive us to the Lemontree Heights cemetery. I shudder thinking of exploring a graveyard. Mom's critters may be creepy, but at least they're alive.

Mom appears in the doorway. Her hair is sticking up at weird angles, and she has purple bags under her eyes.

"I made lunch." I set a plate of sandwiches on the table.

"Where's your brother?"

Why do I always have to keep tabs on Crispy? "I saw him in the barn, playing with Chewbacca." I narrow my brows. Hmmm . . . could my harebrained little brother have something to do with the kitten appearing in Chewbacca's enclosure? And what about the dog collar? I pull the collar out of the pocket of my spy vest. "Look what I found in Chewbacca's pen."

"What now?" Mom sits down at the table. She sighs and slumps down in her chair.

"Are you okay?" I hope she's not working too hard again.

"I have to get back to the clinic." She grabs a sandwich. "A border collie ate a sock and a pair of underpants." She takes a bite. "I have to do surgery to get them out."

What kind of dog eats socks and underwear? You wouldn't believe the stuff Mom has removed from the guts of people's pets—river rocks, rubber bands, stuffed toys, potted plants. But socks and underwear are actually pretty common when it comes to foreign body ingestion. I know how she always worries when animals need surgery. Even though it's routine and totally safe, it's someone's baby she's fixing up. So, I don't want to worry her with Hairy Pawter's dog collar. She's got enough on her mind. "Want a glass of almond milk?"

Mom smiles. "Sure. Thanks, Petunia."

I tighten my lips. I hate it when she calls me that stupid nickname, but I don't say anything. I guess she thinks I'm a flower . . . either that or the cartoon character Petunia Pig. I pour a glass of almond milk and bring it back to the table.

Crispy bursts through the kitchen door. "Look what I found!" He holds up a plaid bandana in one hand and a leash in the other. "Chewbacca had them." The bandana is all stretched out of shape and has teeth marks in it. Chewbacca must have been chewing on it.

I wonder if they belong to Hairy Pawter. *If they do, where is Hairy now? And why are his collar, bandana, and leash in Chewbacca's cage?* The chimp wouldn't have eaten a dog, would she? Nah. Like Crispy, she's a vegetarian, unless you count ants and beetles. "Mom has to remove some underwear from a border collie's stomach. Eat your lunch and don't bug her."

"Aren't we going to the library?" Crispy drops the dog paraphernalia on the table and plops into a chair next to Mom. Freddie jumps off his shoulder and helps himself to a sandwich.

"Freddie!" I should have known I'd have to make a spare.

"Kassy, watch your brother." Mom wipes her hands on a napkin. "I can't take you to the library until after work. Sorry, I have to fish out those underpants."

"Don't forget the sock!" I grin.

After Mom leaves, I pull the old diary out of my spy vest. The back pocket is huge, and it's the perfect place to keep the diary near me . . . and out of the wrong hands.

Speaking of the wrong hands, Freddie leaps across the table and grabs the diary's leather strap in his teeth. "Keep your paws off, stinky!"

Crispy pouts. "Don't call him that. You'll hurt his feelings." He reaches for the ferret. "Besides, he can't help it. He has a bad tummy."

"Yeah, from eating everything in sight." I try to ignore my brother and his thieving ferret and concentrate on the diary. I flip to the page with the riddles. Maybe they lead to the lock that fits the key Freddie found. I stare down at the yellowed parchment. I have the key in its box hidden under my bed. If I can decipher the clues in the diary, maybe I can find the treasure chest and unlock it.

Marking a life lost when firmly in place. An enduring epitaph inscribed on my face. That must be a tombstone. I just have to figure out which tombstone.

I read the next riddle out loud. "'The one that does not belong: Corset, Sector, Escort, Court.'"

"What does that mean?" Crispy asks.

"Good question." I scratch my head. "One of these words doesn't belong in this list. Which is it?" *Holy hypothesis!* I jump up and head for the stairs.

"Where are you going?" Crispy asks with his mouth full of peanut butter sandwich.

"To get my dictionary." I bound up the stairs.

6

THE SECOND RIDDLE

MY BEDROOM IS A CONVERTED ATTIC. It's the only room on the second floor. Like a long, narrow bowling alley with a door at the end, it extends almost the whole length of the house. The ceiling is low and pitched and sometimes I feel like I'm in a tent. With their thick greenish glass, the round windows on either end are like the eyes of some walleyed fish. At dusk, I love to kneel on the window seat with my nose to the glass, spying on the rest of the world below. I can see past the barn and out into the pasture, where Spittoon and Morpheus are grazing.

On my hands and knees, I check under my bed to make sure the box with the key is still there. You never know when

Crispy or Freddie might help himself. The box is safe. Staring at it from this angle, I notice strange grooves on one end. I drag it out from under the bed and run my fingers along the crevasses. The pattern is a circle with teeth. Weird.

I grab my dictionary and run back downstairs.

Crispy is sitting on the floor, munching on a gluten-free chocolate chip cookie and breaking off bits for Freddie, who is perched on his shoulder, as usual.

I plop down next to my brother and crack open the dictionary. I'm going to look up each of the words in the riddle to see if I can figure out which one doesn't belong.

I look up the *C* words first. *Corset: a woman's tightly fitting undergarment, girdle.* I move on to *court.* As I suspected, it has several meanings: a court of law, a tennis or basketball court, a king's court, or *to* court—as in 'to go out with or date.' I hadn't thought of that one.

"What did you find out?" Crispy asks.

"I still have to look up *escort* and *sector.*" I flip to *E. Escort: a person or vehicle accompanying another for protection.* Then I move on to *S. Sector: an area distinct from others, or a mathematical instrument for making diagrams.*

"What do women's girdles, tennis courts, protective vehicles, and mathematical instruments have in common?" I ask, closing the dictionary.

"Aren't we looking for the one that doesn't belong?"

"Right. But we can only figure out what doesn't belong by finding out what *does* belong. If we can learn how these things fit together, then we can see which one doesn't fit." Crispy holds out a baggie of cookies to me, and I take one.

"Maybe it isn't supposed to be a word." Crispy breaks off a piece of cookie and hands it to Freddie, who holds it between his paws and nibbles like a squirrel.

"What do you mean?" I ask.

"It's a riddle, right?" As Crispy talks, I help myself to another cookie from his stash. "So maybe it's about the letters and not the words."

"You mean like an anagram? So we rearrange the letters?"

"Yeah. Or maybe the letters are in code."

"If they're in code, then we need to figure out the key to break it."

Crispy pulls Freddie down from his shoulders and ties the bandana around the ferret's neck.

"It's way too big for him." I hold out my hand. "Can I see that?"

Crispy unties the bandana and hands it to me.

"You found this in Chewy's pen?"

Crispy nods and pulls the leash out from his pocket. "And this, too."

"I wonder if these belong to Hairy Pawter." I finger the leash.

"Harry Potter?" Crispy gets excited.

I pull the dog collar out of my vest pocket. "I found this in Chewbacca's pen earlier. It belongs to a dog named Hairy Pawter. See?" I hand him the collar.

"How do you know it's a dog?"

"Good point. As a detective, I shouldn't make assumptions." I fold the bandana and put it into one of my pockets, along with the leash and the collar. "Who else wears a bandana, a collar, and a leash?"

"You have a case!" Crispy claps his hands together.

"I have too many cases." I stash the diary in my back pocket. "We still have to figure out the riddle and find the treasure so we can save Mrs. Patel's bakery."

"And we have to find Hairy Pawter." When Crispy jumps up off the floor, Freddie squeaks and . . . well, you know. *Phew!*

"Were there always so many pets missing?" I push my glasses back up on my nose—they're forever sliding down. "Or am I only noticing now?"

"What do you mean?" Crispy puts the rest of his cookies in the cupboard.

"Yara was missing. Then I saw flyers for three other dogs. There was that cat in Chewbacca's pen, and now Hairy Pawter."

"Is Chewy a dognapper?"

I shake my head. "Chewbacca would have to sneak in and out of her cage to do that. Two of the missing pets *are* connected to Chewy, but how?" I stand up and wipe my hands off on the butt of my jeans. "And Dad's neighborhood is ten minutes away by car. That's a long way to go on foot, even if you have four feet."

"Maybe the cat snuck into the petting zoo and climbed into Chewy's pen. It's a small cat." Crispy's hair is sticking out in all directions, like he stuck his finger in a light socket.

When I smooth Crispy's hair, Freddie slaps my hand, warning me to keep my paws off his person.

"Maybe so." I check my spy watch. I replaced its battery and it's working again. "I hope Mom gets done soon so we can go to the library and do some research. While we're waiting, I'll go check the bulletin board and see if anyone reported a missing dog named Hairy Pawter."

The doorbell startles me. Crispy and I look at each other. We both head through the living room to the front door. When I peek through the peephole, my heart skips a beat. *What's he doing here?*

Pinkerton Killjoy from Animal Control is not my favorite person. He's always trying to shut down the petting zoo. And after everything that happened last month, he doesn't like me much either.

Before I can stop him, Crispy pulls the door open.

Stinkerton Killjoy stares down at us. "Is your mother at home?"

I think Agent Killjoy has a crush on Mom. And for some reason, she likes him, too . . . but just as a friend, I hope. *Yuck.* I don't even want to think about it.

"She's at work." Crispy points toward the vet clinic.

"Does Lemontree Petting Zoo have any animals missing?" Killjoy trains his beady eyes on me.

"No." I shake my head. "Everyone is accounted for." *At least, I hope so!*

"Are you sure you aren't missing a chimpanzee?" Killjoy tilts his head to look inside the house, as if we're hiding a missing animal inside. "One of your neighbors reported seeing what looked like a chimp rummaging through their trash can last night."

Crispy's eyes get big, and he gives me a questioning look. I scrunch my brows and tighten my lips in warning. He'd better not say anything to Killjoy about Chewbacca's cat visitor or Hairy Pawter's accessories.

"Chewy—"

I step on Crispy's toes before he can finish the sentence. This kid can't take a hint.

"Chewbacca, our chimp, is in her enclosure," I say. "The neighbor probably saw a bear or a dog."

Killjoy strokes his mustache. "You'd better be right. The next time an animal escapes from Lemontree Petting Zoo, I'll close you down so fast you won't know what hit you."

I don't understand why Mom likes this guy. With friends like this, who needs enemies?

Freddie gives Killjoy the business end and toots in protest.

"Stinking rodent," Killjoy says, adjusting his hat.

"Freddie is not a rodent!" Crispy hugs Freddie close to his chest. "Ferrets are polecats in the weasel family."

"The scientific name is *Mustela putorius furo*," I add for emphasis. "Not *Rodentia*." With his pointy nose and close-set eyes, Killjoy is the one who looks like a rodent. "Forty percent of all mammal species may be rodents, but Flatulent Freddie's not one of them."

Crispy gives me a dirty look. But if the shoe fits . . . Not that ferrets wear shoes, unless Crispy has been stealing my American Girl doll shoes and socks (and underpants!) again to dress the animals.

"You two take the cake." Killjoy shakes his head. "The apple doesn't fall far from the tree. Like father like daughter."

"Thanks for the compliments." Under my breath, I add, "Stinkerton," then flash a big fake smile. Killjoy is just jealous because Mom married Dad instead of him.

He sighs. "I mean it. If another one of your animals gets out, you're done for!" He turns on his heels and stomps off across the grass toward his yellow van.

"Good riddance!" When I slam the door shut, Freddie squeals.

"He's not going to shut us down, is he?" Crispy's voice cracks. I hope he isn't going to start crying.

"Don't worry. Your animal friends are safe."

"Promise?" Crispy looks up at me, his eyes glowing with fear.

"I promise." I put one arm around him, but I cross my fingers behind my back just in case.

7

LYNCOYA JACKSON'S SECRETS

WAITING FOR MOM TO FINISH AT THE CLINIC, I curl up on the window seat in my bedroom, reading Lyncoya's diary. It's pretty interesting stuff. He's really into horses, which makes sense given he works at a saddle shop.

On a page in the middle of the diary, Lyncoya writes, "Father carries a bullet next to his heart for Truxton." *Who is Truxton? Is that another riddle?* Maybe *bullet* is just a figure of speech, and his father has a pain in his heart for this Truxton person. I wonder if I have a bullet next to my heart. It hasn't stopped hurting since Dad left. Mom tells me it's not my fault . . . but it still hurts.

Mom opens my bedroom door and pokes her head in. "You're supposed to be watching your brother."

"You're supposed to knock."

Mom scowls. "If you still want to go to the library, you'd better get moving."

The Lemontree Heights Public Library is one of my favorite places. I love the musty smell of books, especially old books. Mom loves the library, too. She heads for the mystery and thriller section. I like the middle-grade shelf. It's in the kids' section, which is big, bright, and colorful. And the little kids' corner is separated off from the older kids, which I like since little kids can be so noisy.

I head for the computers to search for information on Andrew Jackson and Lyncoya.

Crispy and Freddie head for the plate of butter cookies in the kids' section. I know—there shouldn't be food in a library, but Lemontree Heights isn't your ordinary library. Anyway, the librarian, Mrs. Bompvaudle, doesn't allow the little kids and their cookies to trespass in other sections of the library, but she never shushes them.

With her stern bun and pointy glasses, Mrs. Bompvaudle looks scary, but she's not at all scary when you get to know her. She has a sign on her desk that reads, "Books are more fun than TV or videogames. Try one!" Once, I asked her why she let the little kids make so much noise, and she said she didn't want to be like her mother, who used to tell her, "Children should speak when chickens pee," which I thought was pretty funny since chickens don't pee.

All of the computers are being used, so I take a number and wait my turn. Pacing back and forth behind the computer table, I glance at my spy watch. *Brussels sprouts!* The library closes in a half hour. If a computer doesn't free up soon, it will be a wasted trip . . . at least for me.

Not for Crispy. He's sitting in the foyer pulling butter cookies out of his pocket and sharing them with Freddie. Believe it or not, Mrs. Bompvaudle allows Crispy to bring his ferret into the library. She says Freddie is my brother's "emotional support animal." I say Crispy is the ferret's emotional support human.

"You're going to wear a hole in the carpet pacing like that." Mrs. Bompvaudle startles me. "Can I help you with something?"

"I'm waiting for one of the computers to open up."

"Unless you're looking for the best ice cream shop in Lemontree Heights or shopping for cat food online, I bet we can find what you need in a book." Mrs. Bompvaudle raises her eyebrows. "So what is it you're looking for?"

"Information about Lyncoya Jackson—"

"Andrew Jackson's adopted son." Mrs. Bompvaudle smiles. She's the reference librarian, and she's better than any computer. "Found on the battlefield . . . so sad."

"Why sad?" I ask.

She crooks her finger at me and heads toward the reference section. Once we leave the carpet, her stubby-heeled shoes tap on the tiled floor. I skip to keep up. Even in her tight skirt, she walks fast.

"Poor kid." She stops in front of a shelf of fat encyclopedias, lined up and standing at attention like a platoon. She runs her finger across the volumes until she reaches the letter *J*. She slides one of the thick volumes from the shelf, licks her finger, and flips through the pages. "Jackson," she says under her breath. She smiles in triumph as she hands the volume to me, opened to the entry on Andrew Jackson.

"Andrew Jackson was called 'Old Hickory' because he was as tough as hardwood." She tightens her lips. "He was not a nice man."

The encyclopedia is heavy in my hands. "He adopted Lyncoya. That's nice." I glance up at Mrs. B.

"He picked up the poor orphaned infant off the battle-field after he'd wiped out the boy's entire family." She sniffs. "Andrew Jackson made his name as a soldier." The way she says *soldier* makes me think she has a different word in mind.

"Wasn't he the president?"

"Lots of presidents were soldiers first. And just because he was president doesn't mean he was nice." Mrs. B. adjusts her glasses. "He had slaves. He killed Native Americans. He drank and gambled. He even fought in duels."

Crispy and Freddie appear out of nowhere. "You mean with pistols?" Crispy asks.

"Yes. He was shot several times and survived." When Mrs. B. pets Freddie's snout with her finger, the ferret makes a purring sound. You'd think he was a cat.

"'My father has a bullet near his heart . . .'" I remember the line from Lyncoya's diary. "So maybe it wasn't a figure of speech. Maybe it was a real bullet."

Crispy's eyes widen.

"But who is Truxton?" I whisper.

I carry the fat encyclopedia over to a nearby table and slide into a chair. Crispy, Freddie, and Mrs. B follow me. Using my index finger as a pointer, I skim the page for clues.

"Does it describe the famous duel?" Mrs. B asks, a knowing smile on her face.

I skate my finger over the words. *There it is!* The word *duel. Chicken-fried steak!* Andrew Jackson fought lots of duels. He killed a man over a racehorse named Truxton and got shot himself. *Bingo!* That must be the bullet close to his heart.

Mrs. B was right. Andrew Jackson was a gambler. He raised racehorses and bet on them. On the next page, there's a painting of a thin man with white hair wearing a soldier's riding jacket and tall black boots atop a white horse. "President Andrew Jackson on Little Sorrel," I read out loud. The pretty horse with the long mane has sad eyes.

"What does it say?" Crispy asks, leaning over my shoulder.

"Lyncoya must have grown up taking care of the stables at Andrew Jackson's plantation outside Nashville. Aside from cotton, their main crop was horses, especially racehorses."

"That's why he worked in a saddle shop!" Crispy sounds proud of himself.

"Thank you, Captain Obvious."

A woman's voice comes over the loudspeaker: "The library will be closing in ten minutes."

"Time to wrap it up." Mrs. B. waves her hand over the encyclopedia. "But before you go, let me get you a biography of Andrew Jackson. Your mom can check it out for you."

"Thanks, Mrs. B." I speed-read the rest of the entry. He was the seventh president, a lawyer, and a soldier. He once beat a would-be assassin with his walking stick. He had a talking African gray parrot named Poll, who cursed so loud he had to be removed from Jackson's own funeral service. But Jackson's main passion was horses and horseracing.

Thinking about horses makes me miss my dad. Before he moved out, we had a horse ranch. After Dad left, Mom sold it and started the petting zoo. Morpheus the pony is the only horse we have now.

A picture of a sleek chestnut brown horse with a black mane catches my eye. The caption reads "Truxton." *Aha!* The racehorse Lyncoya's father fought over.

"The library will be closing in five minutes." The voice over the loudspeaker startles me.

I quickly flip through the pages looking for an entry on Lyncoya Jackson.

Mrs. B sits down next to me. "Time to put the encyclopedia away. The library is closing," she says softly. "Here's the biography. You can read it at home."

"Just one more minute." My heart racing, I skim the page.

Slug was right. Lyncoya was a Creek Native American born in 1811. He died of tuberculosis in 1828 at the age of seventeen, only three years older than that new boy, Slug.

Whoa! Mrs. B was right. Andrew Jackson found Lyncoya on a battlefield after he'd killed the baby's entire family. He took the orphan home to his wife, Rachel, and they raised him as their own. *Wouldn't it be weird knowing your adoptive father killed your whole family?* I shudder just thinking about it.

8

THE MISSING COCKAPOO

THE NEXT DAY, MOM DROPS US OFF at the bakery bright and early before she opens the vet clinic. It's only seven in the morning, and already Mrs. Patel has been baking for hours. As I open the back door to the bakery, the sweet and spicy smells of cinnamon and cardamom hit my nose. Immediately, I start craving a cup of creamy spiced chai.

Mrs. Patel wipes her hands on her apron and smiles. "I have a special treat for you today." She gestures for us to come closer. With her hands in thick oven mitts, she pulls a giant pan of perfect round golden cookies from the oven. She removes the mitts and snaps on latex gloves, then sprinkles a pinch of ground cashews with coconut of top of each cookie. "They're called *nankhatai.*"

"Indian shortbread cookies," Butler adds.

"They smell delicious." My mouth waters.

"Can we try them?" Crispy asks. His eyes are open wide.

"Booboo, bring me a plate." Mrs. Patel nods at Butler.

Butler scrunches his eyebrows, and I try not to laugh.

"You kids can try them with some chai." Using a spatula, Mrs. P lifts a dozen cookies off the sheet and gently sets them on the plate. One cookie slides off the spatula onto the floor, and before you can say "Booboo," Freddie leaps down from Crispy's shoulders and scarfs it.

"Booboo, take the cookies into the storage room before the health inspector sees Freddie and shuts me down," Mrs. P chuckles. "I have enough trouble as it is."

"He's Lucy's emotional support animal," I say.

Mrs. P just shakes her head.

Butler carries the plate of cookies out of the kitchen and around the corner to the storage closet. Crispy, Freddie, and I follow him. He puts the plate on top of one of the cardboard boxes. "Who wants chai?"

"Me!" Crispy and I say in unison.

Butler—*Booboo*—disappears and reappears a minute later carrying a tray. We each take a cup of steaming spicy tea and then dig into the cookies.

Yummy! This is my kind of breakfast. Not like the gluten-free oatmeal we get at home.

Inside the cluttered storage room, we sit on boxes and munch on cookies.

"Did you figure out what that key is to?" Butler asks between bites.

"No. But we figured out one of the riddles from Lyncoya's diary." I dip the edge of a cookie into my tea. "And I think once we solve all the riddles, we'll find the lock that goes with this key. But first we have to find a tombstone. Do you think your brother could drive us to the cemetery later?"

"The cemetery?" Butler narrows his eyes

I slide the diary out of my spy vest. "The clue to the treasure is..." I flip to the back of the diary. "'Marking a life lost, when firmly in place. An enduring epitaph, inscribed on my face.' It's a tombstone."

"Even if you find this tombstone, what then?"

"We find the treasure and save the bakery!" Crispy pumps his fist in the air, and Freddie squeaks.

"How do you know there's a treasure?" Butler crosses his legs and sips his tea.

"Gut feeling." I take the last cookie from the plate.

"If there's a treasure, Kassy will find it." Crispy jabs the air for effect.

"Thanks for the vote of confidence." I break the cookie into thirds and offer a piece to my brother and to Butler.

"I hope you're not planning to dig up a grave." Butler raises his eyebrows.

"I hadn't thought of that." *Gross!* I shudder at the idea of digging up a grave.

"Maybe we should get Dad's old shovel from the garage." Crispy sounds excited about the possibility of grave digging.

"Not all treasures are buried." I hope this one isn't . . . at least not in a graveyard.

The bells on the front door jingle, signaling the first customer of the day. "I'd better go help my mom." Butler brushes his hands together and stands up.

"I'll come with you." I turn to Crispy. "Why don't you stay here. We don't want Freddie scaring off the customers."

My brother glares at me. "Freddie couldn't scare a fly."

"Only because he eats them before they know what's hit them." When I ruffle Crispy's hair, he jerks his head away.

I follow Butler down the short hallway to the storefront, where Mrs. Patel has loaded the bakery case with trays of desserts. There are *gulab jamun* and mango puddings in individual tart tins, rice puddings with pistachios, and, my favorite, milk barfi.

A paunchy man with a handlebar mustache stands at the cash register chatting with Mrs. Patel.

"Hairy didn't come home last night," the man sniffs. "I'm worried about him."

Mrs. Patel shakes her head.

"I couldn't sleep for worrying." The man stuffs his hands into the pockets of his trousers. "It's not like him to stay out all night."

"Don't worry. He'll come back." Mrs. Patel smiles. "Would you like some chai and a fresh-baked cookie?" She turns to Butler. "Boo, please get Mr. Swindell some chai." She scoots out from behind the cash register and leads Mr. Swindell to a café table. "A nice cup of chai will make you feel better."

I watch from the counter as Butler delivers two cups of tea and a small plate of cookies. I'm dying to know who this 'Hairy' is and why he didn't come home last night.

Mr. Swindell slumps into a chair. His body overflows its delicate metal frame, and he looks like a cupcake balancing on a toothpick. I hope he doesn't fall off. He picks up a cookie and sighs. "Poor Hairy. I hope he's not hurt . . . or worse." He pops the whole cookie into his mouth. When he chews, he looks like a cow with its cud.

"Mr. Swindell, I've been meaning to talk to you about the rent." Mrs. Patel sips her tea. "You see, the thing is, business has been a bit slow, and—"

Aha! Mr. Swindell must be the landlord.

"I've just got to find Hairy. Poor little guy out there all alone." He shakes his egg-shaped head. "He always comes when I call him, but not last night."

"Excuse me, Mr. Swindell." Butler pours creamy tea from a pitcher to top off their cups. "May I ask, who is Harry?"

Mr. Swindell looks up from the table. "Hairy Pawter, my dog."

Cheese and rice! The collar! I make my way past the cash register and into the storefront. "Hairy Pawter is your dog?"

"Yes. Have you seen him?" Mr. Swindell perks up.

"What does he look like?" I pull my notebook from the pocket of my spy vest.

"He's a caramel-colored cockapoo." Mr. Swindell takes his phone from his shirt pocket and taps it awake. "Here he is." He shows me a picture of a shaggy dog with curly orange hair, floppy ears, a black gumdrop nose, and its tongue hanging out.

I stare at the picture for a few seconds trying to discern any identifying features. "When did you see him last?" I put pen to paper.

"I was walking him yesterday afternoon. Someone set off fireworks and he bolted."

"Kassy is a pet detective." Crispy appears out of nowhere. "She'll find your dog."

My eyes widen as Freddie peeks up over Crispy's mop of hair. The ferret is standing on Crispy's shoulders, paws on top of my brother's head. Without Mr. Swindell noticing, I signal my brother to hide Freddie. I doubt the landlord will like a rodent on his property...well *we* know Freddie isn't a rodent, but he doesn't.

I stand in between Crispy and Mr. Swindell, blocking his view of the ferret. "I think we have a lead on Hairy Pawter." I remove the dog paraphernalia from my spy vest. "Do these belong to Hairy?"

Mr. Swindell's face lights up. "Why yes. Where'd you get those?" He reaches for the collar. "But—wait. Where's Hairy?" His face falls. "Why do you have his leash and collar? And his bandana?"

"We found them near our place." I don't want to tell Mr. Swindell about the collar and leash being found *inside* the petting zoo until I know what's going on.

"Oh no! Poor Hairy!" Mr. Swindell looks panicked. "He slipped out of his collar, leash, and bandana? How is that possible?"

I don't tell him my theory about a petnapper . . . or that our chimp likes to dress and undress dogs.

"Where do you live? Maybe if I come out and call him, he'll come." Mr. Swindell's eyes are watering. I wonder if he's going to start crying.

"We live just on the edge of town, about a mile away. Lemontree Petting Zoo."

"I heard about a dog who crossed the country, like a thousand miles, to get back home," Crispy says.

"I'm offering a reward if you find him."

"Kassy doesn't accept rewards," Crispy volunteers.

Unless I need to collect rewards in order to save the bakery! I scowl at Crispy.

"I'd owe you big time if you return my Hairy to me." Mr. Swindell looks so sad. He must really love his dog.

"Is that the collar and leash we found in Chewy's . . . " Crispy steps forward and I scoot in front of him again.

I cut off Crispy before he spills the beans about Chewbacca. "I'll take the case."

"If anyone can find Hairy Pawter, Kassy will." Butler smiles at me as he refills the tea cups again.

At least the missing dog will distract Mr. Swindell from the missing rent... and the ferret. And maybe if I find Hairy Pawter, he will give Mrs. Patel a break. It's worth a try. Anyway, I have to find out what's going on with Chewbacca. Something fishy is going on, and I'm going to find out what.

"Did you contact Animal Control?" I hate to think of going to Animal Control and running into Stinkerton Killjoy. "Maybe they picked up Hairy."

"Not there. I checked."

"Did you post something online?" Butler asks.

"Yeah. I put Hairy's picture on the neighborhood list."

If Mom would let me have a cell phone or use her computer, my job would be a lot easier.

"Nobody's seen him anywhere." Mr. Swindell inhales another cookie, then stands up. "I'm going to drive out to Lemontree Petting Zoo and see if I can find him. I just don't know what I'd do if anything happens to Hairy."

"Don't worry, Mr. Swindell." I slip my notebook and pen back into my pocket. "We'll find him."

The bells on the front door jingle as he leaves.

Freddie jumps off my brother's shoulders and races for the cookie Mr. Swindell left on the plate. Crispy runs after him—or maybe he's lunging for the cookie, too. "Chewbacca knows where to find Hairy Pawter." He scoops the ferret into his arms and holds him like a baby.

Freddie nibbles the cookie between his paws. I have to admit—my brother and his ferret are kind of cute in a weirdo sort of way.

"Chewbacca?" Mrs. P asks.

"Chewy, our chimp," Crispy says.

"Sorry I asked." She busies herself with the cash drawer.

"We need to question Chewy," Crispy says.

"What makes you think she'll answer?" I ask.

"She answers me."

I shake my head. "I'm not fluent in chimp."

"I'll translate for you!" Crispy rocks Freddie in his arms. "Maybe Spittoon can track Hairy down." He pulls the bandana out of my back pocket. "Look. We can use this to give Spittoon his scent."

"Spittoon the bloodhound camel." I roll my eyes. Sometimes I think my brother is a few sandwiches short of a picnic. But at this point, interviewing Chewbacca and putting Spittoon on the scent might be our best options.

Out the window, I see Mr. Swindell posting flyers offering a reward for his missing dog. He's taping sheets of paper to every telephone and lamppost on Main Street. I should take one and put it on the bulletin board at Mom's clinic.

Oh no! Not him! Slug is heading for the entrance to the bakery. *What's he doing here?*

I dash back into the storage closet and listen at the door. I can barely make out the voices.

"James, do your parents know you're here?" Mrs. Patel asks.

"I don't have parents," Slug answers.

"Don't say that." Mrs. Patel's voice is gentle. "I'm sure your parents love you and worry about you. Would you like a cookie? They're fresh baked."

"Sure. Thanks."

"Boo, will you get James a plate of cookies from the kitchen?"

I peek my head out of the closet and wave at Butler. "What's he doing here?"

"He comes in every day," Butler says on his way to the kitchen. "Looking for you." Butler gets that hangdog look on his face. I guess, like me, he's not a fan of Slug.

What? Sure enough, I hear Slug asking, "Is Kassy here today?"

Crispy pipes up. "She's in her office."

Thanks a lot, traitor! I duck back into the storage closet, quietly shut the door, and hide behind a stack of boxes.

Even from my hiding place, I hear Slug say, "Kassy broke her promise to meet me here last week, and I don't like liars."

Cringe. I totally forgot about meeting Slug.

"She thinks she's such a great pet detective. Ha! I'll show her who's a great detective!"

What? Does he have a picture of Sherlock Holmes? I stick my tongue out at him from behind the boxes.

I hear the bell on the front door jingle.

"She'll regret ghosting me!" Slug shouts.

9
THE CEMETERY

MRS. PATEL GIVES SLUG MORE TREATS and sends him on his way. *Good.* I don't want him butting into my treasure hunt.

Butler, Crispy, and I spend the rest of the morning helping Mrs. P at the bakery. I sweep the floors. Butler sprinkles saffron on the puddings. Crispy and Freddie . . . well, you could say, they're the taste testers. Freddie also helps clean. Whenever a cookie or donut falls on the floor, he's right there to scarf it up. No wonder he's getting a potbelly.

After helping Mrs. P in the kitchen, waiting on a few customers, and cleaning the storefront windows, we've run out of chores. Butler pulls out a deck of cards.

We're sitting at one of the café tables, playing a game of Go Fish, when Mrs. P offers us lunch—three spicy curries, fragrant jasmine rice, and *naan* flatbread served in metal bowls. We each take a metal plate divided with ridges to keep the curries separate . . . like a school cafeteria tray, only not plastic.

"Um, Mrs. Patel?" Crispy says. "Is there any meat in here?" He points to the bowls. "I don't eat animals."

"Don't worry, Percy. Neither do I." Mrs. P puts the steaming bowls on one of the small tables.

"Cool!" Crispy helps himself to vegetable curry and rice.

Butler pushes the other two tiny tables together.

After I dish up my plate, I join the others at the tables, and dig in. The lunch is warm and spicy. Usually, I don't like spinach, but this creamed spinach with cheese is pretty yummy.

"So how are you going to find Hairy Pawter?" Crispy asks.

"I'm going to ask Chewy, like you said."

Butler takes out his phone. "Nothing yet on the neighborhood list."

The bells jingle on the front door. Butler's older brother, Oliver, saunters in. Oliver is seventeen, has a ponytail, and wears loose jeans. Most importantly, he has a driver's license. His short-sleeve shirt reveals a tattoo on his forearm. When I strain to see what it is, I can make out a small black wing.

"Oli, there's lunch if you want some." Mrs. Patel gestures toward the table chock-full of food.

"Thanks, Mom." Oliver grins. "I never turn down food." He loads up a plate with so much rice it looks like a white mountain surrounded by a lake of curry.

I wait until Mrs. Patel goes back into the kitchen, and then I ask Oliver, "Will you drive us to the cemetery?"

"The cemetery?" Oliver laughs. "Aren't you too young to hang out there?"

"And too alive," Butler adds. "Which cemetery?"

"There's more than one?" I ask. *Deep-fried okra!* It could take forever to find the right headstone.

"We found a treasure map in the wall, and the first clue leads to a tombstone," Crispy says, bouncing up and down on his chair.

I pull the diary from my vest and flip to the page with the riddles. "The one that does not belong," I read aloud. "Corset, Sector, Escort, Court."

"Let me see that," Oliver says with his mouth full.

I scowl. I don't want him to get curry all over my antique diary . . . I mean, it's not exactly *my* diary, but I'm holding onto it for safekeeping. I hold the page out where he can see it.

"Anagrams," he says, taking another giant bite of naan.

"I told you!" Crispy jumps up and down. Freddie toots in protest.

"That rodent stinks!" Oliver closes his eyes and scrunches up his nose. "He's ruining my lunch."

"Freddie can't help it." Crispy caresses the ferret's furry head.

"Can't you put a plug in it?" Oliver chuckles and waves his hand in front of his face. "Do you want my mom's bakery to get shut down? Next time leave the rodent at home."

Crispy tucks Freddie inside his shirt and pouts.

"Anagrams." I ignore them and concentrate on the words: *Corset, Sector, Escort, Court.*

"All but one," Crispy says. "Anagrams are words made by rearranging the letters—"

"Court!" *That's it!* I take out my notebook, write *COURT*, and circle the *U*. "All of the other words have the same letters, except for the *U* in *court*."

"Very clever, Carrot." Oliver scrapes the last of the curry up with his bread and pops it into his mouth.

I frown. "I'm not a root vegetable."

"Carrottop, then." He flashes his crooked-toothed grin.

"Ha ha! Very funny. *Not*."

"All of the words are anagrams of the others, except for *court*!" Butler smiles. "Wow. So cool."

"But what does it mean?" Crispy asks. "What court?"

"That's what we're going to the cemetery to find out."

Oliver narrows his eyes. "I'm not following. What does court have to do with the cemetery?"

"The answer to the first riddle is tombstone. So, if we go to the cemetery and look at the headstones, maybe we'll find court . . . maybe Court is a proper name." My heart speeds up. "We need to find a gravestone for someone named Court."

"Wow! I like the way your brain works." Butler smiles at me.

"Cool!" Oliver gets up from the table. "Let's clean this up, and then we can go." He picks up the tray and starts stacking the empty dishes on it. "Can't wait," he chuckles. "Another adventure with Carrot O'Roarke."

I tighten my lips but don't say anything. I guess being called Carrot is the price I pay for hitching a ride to the cemetery.

The first cemetery on my list is on the outskirts of Lemontree Heights, just past our house and next to a forest preserve, which makes it isolated and extra creepy. A tall wrought iron fence encloses the graveyard on three sides, making me think of the animal enclosures in our petting zoo. *Is the fence to keep undead zombies in or local hoodlums out?*

Three flags atop towering poles flap in the breeze: the US flag, the Tennessee state flag, and a green-and-yellow flag with a tree on it, the Lemontree Heights flag. As we drive through the

giant metal gate, shivers run up my spine. I've actually never been in a graveyard before. At least the afternoon sun is bright and warm. I can't imagine coming here at night. And there are hundreds of tombstones. Checking them all will take days.

Oliver parks the car in the designated lot at the entrance. There's not a soul in sight. *Hmmm . . . maybe I shouldn't say* soul *in a cemetery.* I'm not sure what a soul would look like, especially disconnected from a body. I'm not eager to find out, either.

"Fan out and search the headstones for someone named Court," I command the troops.

In spite of the warm breeze, I feel cold. I wrap my spy vest tighter around my chest. Walking on tiptoe, I head into the cemetery, careful to stay on the path. Something about the graveyard makes me want to be very quiet and sneaky.

On either side of the path, flat stone markers are etched with names and dates. Some thick granite stones stand three feet high and are carved with inscriptions. *Beloved wife and mother. Korean war veteran and beloved father.* I stop in front of a small plaque nested near a large stone. The plaque has a picture of a cherub drawn on it. Fresh flowers stand in a vase nearby. *Someone must miss their baby a lot.* I wonder if Mom would put flowers on my grave every day.

I glance around the cemetery. To read all the headstones, I'll have to venture out onto the grass. I wonder if that's okay. I take a couple of steps into the grass, then look around again to see if anyone's busted me.

Crispy and Freddie are racing down one path and then another, like rats in a maze. Back in the parking lot, Oliver is leaning against the car, looking cool. I don't see Butler.

I continue tiptoeing along the path, reading the headstones as I go. I wish they were in alphabetical order. That would make it a lot easier.

The gravel on the path crunches under my sandals. I try to walk without making any noise.

Clumps of evergreen trees stand gathered around some of the graves, and bushes with white flowers cordon off those of whole families. Just ahead on the path to my right, a statue of an angel with folded wings overlooks several stones.

I don't know if it's the heat or my nerves, but my palms are sweating. I wipe them on my shorts. I'm glad I'm wearing my fedora to shield my eyes from the glaring sun. It's the hottest part of the afternoon, and the humidity is playing tricks on my eyes. The wind picks up, making the plants dance and the trees sway. The flags whip and crack. A whirling sound in the distance makes me swing around and stare across the graves. *Weird.* I feel like I'm being watched.

Something warm touches my shoulder. "Brussels sprouts, Butler!" My hands fly to my chest. "You almost gave me a heart attack."

"Sorry." Butler shrugs. "Did you find Court?"

"Not yet." Once I get over my surprise, I'm kind of glad he's here. Wandering through this graveyard alone is nerve-racking.

I try to ignore my fears and continue on my mission. It could take all day to read all these headstones. Maybe I'm wrong and the riddles don't point to a tombstone with the name Court. I wipe sweat off my forehead.

A shadow runs across the open grass. I hold my breath. *Is someone else here? Was that Crispy?* I look around. *No.* Crispy and Freddie are sitting in the shade of a big oak tree near the entrance.

"Did you see that?" I ask Butler.

He shakes his head. "See what?"

I must be imagining things. Maybe the heat is getting to me.

I pull my mini water bottle from my pocket and take a swig. Mom says I have a peaches-and-cream complexion, but when I get hot, it's more like beets-and-cottage-cheese.

A dog barks in the distance, and then a whole chorus of barking echoes through the trees. But I don't see any dogs. *Do ghost dogs bark?*

I take another sip of water and continue down the path toward a small brick building at the edge of the cemetery. It must be some kind of administration building. Maybe there is an attendant who can help us

I glimpse a shadow zip behind the building. It moved faster than humanly possible. "Did you see that?" I ask Butler again, who's still tagging along behind me.

"See what?"

"Something just zoomed behind that building." I shield my eyes and stare into the distance.

"Maybe we should get out of here." Butler wipes his forehead with the back of his hand. "This place gives me the creeps."

Shih tzu puppy! My heart leaps. I definitely see someone whizzing down the lane behind the administration building. "Come on!" I stuff my water bottle back in my pocket and take off running. The figure is moving so fast it's like he's on wheels. *Wait!* He *is* on wheels—a skateboard!

I'm gaining on him, but he's going too fast. As I get closer, I recognize his slouch. "Slug!" I yell at the top of my lungs. "Wait."

Slug wheels around on his board, kicks up its end, and grabs it. "Kassandra? What are you doing here?" He runs his fingers through his curly brown hair.

I scowl. Does he think he's my mother, calling me by my whole name? "I was about to ask you the same question." I double over to catch my breath.

"Hey, Slug." Butler catches up to us. "Nice board."

Slug nods.

"Were you following us?" I ask, panting.

"I'm on my way home."

"I thought you didn't have a home." I yank my hat off and fan myself with it.

"I'm like a bird, remember?" Slug grins. "I live in the trees." He points toward the forest with his board.

I narrow my eyes at him. "You live in the forest?"

"Do you live in that creepy shack?" Crispy appears out of nowhere.

I wonder how he knows about the creepy shack in the middle of the forest preserve. He's not allowed off our property, and it's a long ways through our pastures and the forest to that shack. Technically, I'm not allowed off the property either. But that's where Crispy hid our cougar cub, Apollo, and where I got trapped with a bunch of scary bats . . . it's a long story.

"Yeah. That's right." Slug chuckles. "Wanna come over for tea?"

"You live in that mansion on top of the hill over there." Butler points at a humongous house in the distance. "My mom says your parents—"

"That's the haunted house," I interrupt. As far as I can remember, nobody has lived there except for ghosts. I've never been brave enough to check it out. Does Slug really live in that haunted mansion?

"Maybe I'm a ghost," Slug says, reading my mind. "Boo!" He lunges at me.

I scream and nearly pee my pants. "Knock it off."

"Let's get out of here." Butler pushes his floppy hair out of his eyes and then stuffs his hands in his pockets.

"Yeah, I'm hungry," Crispy chimes in.

"Fetch!" Slug pulls a dog biscuit out of his pocket and throws it into the woods.

Oh no! Freddie jumps off Crispy's shoulders and tears down the path after the biscuit. In two seconds flat, he's out of sight.

"Freddie!" Crispy takes off after him. Before I know it, both have disappeared into the forest.

"Crispy!" I sprint down the path and into the trees. I hear rustling up ahead, but I don't see either of them. Mom will have kittens when she learns I let Crispy out of my sight, especially in the creepy forest next to the cemetery.

With shadows dancing in the breeze and weird bird calls, the forest is even creepier than the cemetery. The path narrows

into an animal trail full of exposed roots and stones. In this heat, even the ground is sweating, and a cloud of humidity floats through the trees like dragon breath.

A shriek pierces my ears. *Oh no! What if Crispy is hurt?* I break into a run. The screaming gets louder. It doesn't sound human. I trip over a root and crash to the ground. My head is spinning, and I feel like I might barf. I can't get up. All I can do is lie there, listening to the desperate screeches and trying not to cry.

10
FREDDIE, PLEASE COME HOME!

AFTER I RECOVER FROM MY FALL, which injured my pride more than my ankle, we continue our search. The screaming stops—I don't know if that's a good or bad sign. I find Crispy sitting under a tree bawling his head off. I pull some tissues from my spy vest and wipe his nose. Seeing him like this makes me sad, too.

After over an hour of searching, there's still no sign of Freddie. Mom will have kittens if we're not home soon. Even Oliver has joined the search.

We spread out and take different quadrants of the forest. I make Crispy come with me. I've already lost Freddie, I'm not losing him too.

Crispy's shoulders are shaking and his voice cracks as he shouts, "Freddie, come boy."

I take my emergency granola bar from the pocket of my spy vest and rattle the wrapper. Freddie loves granola bars almost as much as he does dog biscuits. "Freddie." *Please, Freddie, please come back.* I don't know what Crispy will do without his furry friend—although, technically, ferrets have hair and not fur.

Crispy is full-on crying now. I put my arm around him. His sobs are contagious, but for his sake, I stifle my tears.

"It will be okay. We'll find him." I say it with more confidence than I feel. *Poor Freddie.* He's not used to being on his own. Poor Crispy's not used to being on his own, either.

We reconvene at the administration building inside the cemetery at five sharp as planned. Everyone is hot and tired, and no one has seen any sign of Freddie. *Weird.* Usually that ferret is glued to Crispy like a flea on a dog.

"I'm sorry I threw the biscuit," Slug says. "That was stupid of me."

"True." For once, Slug and I agree on something.

"What if Freddie gets eaten by a wolf or a bear?" Crispy bawls.

"There aren't any wolves or bears in Lemontree Heights." I hand another tissue to Crispy and try not to look worried. There may not be wolves or bears, but there *are* foxes and owls and bobcats—and who knows what else—that might like a fat ferret for dinner.

"We'd better get home before Mom comes looking for us." I try to steer my brother toward the car.

"I'm not leaving until we find Freddie!" Crispy takes off running.

"Crispy, come back!" *Not again* . . . That kid is going to get us all in trouble.

"I'll get him." Slug dashes into the forest after him.

"What am I going to do?" I say more to myself than anyone else.

"Don't worry," Butler says. "You'll find Freddie."

"How? We've been searching for almost two hours."

"You're a pet detective," Butler says. "You just need to focus. You'll look for clues and find Freddie."

"Clues," I repeat. Butler's right. I've got to calm down and think. *What kind of clues would help me find Freddie? Paw prints? Scat? Claw marks? Where do ferrets like to hide? Tree trunks? Holes in the ground? Freddie likes places with dog biscuits and Nerf footballs. And he likes to ride on my brother's shoulders. So where is he now?*

Oliver leans against the front door of the administration building. "We have to get back to the bakery to help Mom close up." He adjusts his baseball cap. "Sorry about your brother's guinea pig."

"Ferret," Butler and I say in unison.

"Jinx." Butler pokes me in the arm, but I'm not in the mood for jokes.

What the . . . Slug is coming out of the forest, carrying my brother over his shoulder like a fireman. Crispy is kicking and screaming.

"Got him," Slug pants. "Where do you want him?"

"I'm not leaving," Crispy shouts.

"Better take him to the car." I lead the way.

I open the door to the back seat. "You'd better get in first," I say to Butler. "Put Crispy in the middle so he can't escape."

Butler climbs into the car. Slug deposits Crispy in the back seat, and I jump in before he can take off again.

"I'll stay here and look for your ferret." Slug salutes us and jogs back to the building, where he left his skateboard leaning against the wall.

"Slug will find Freddie." At least, I'm praying he does. The sun will set in another two hours, and who knows what could happen to Freddie in the forest overnight? I swallow hard.

Oliver drops us off before heading back to the bakery. Crispy folds his arms over his chest and scowls the whole drive home.

"Thanks for the ride." I grab Crispy by the arm and drag him out of the car. "Come on. Mom will know how to find Freddie."

Butler waves from the back seat as Oliver spins out on the gravel in our driveway. *What a show-off.* Mom isn't going to like that bald spot left in the dirt.

Luckily, Mom is still in the clinic. She must have had an emergency surgery. Maybe she had to remove more underwear from the stomach of another nutty dog.

I haul Crispy into the bathroom and clean him up. He's covered in leaves and dirt. I know he must really be upset because he lets me wipe his face with a warm washcloth. I wish Ronny was here to distract him with her soccer ball. I need something to take his mind off Freddie.

"Let's go wait for Mom." I head for the kitchen with Crispy in tow. "Want some cookies while we wait?" Technically, we're not supposed to eat cookies before dinner, but this seems like an emergency.

I guide Crispy into a chair at the kitchen table, then go fish out the bag of gluten-free cookies from the cupboard. They taste like cardboard. But Crispy and Freddie love them. *Poor Freddie . . .*

I hold the bag out to Crispy, but he just shakes his head. With his eyes all red and swollen, and his face even paler than usual, he looks like an albino bat. *Eek! Don't think about bats.* I wrinkle my nose.

I check my spy watch. Six o'clock already. Mom must be removing an entire wardrobe from some St. Bernard.

The kitchen door swings open. "Whew. Sorry I'm so late." *Speak of the deviled egg.* Mom kicks off her shoes and slides toward the refrigerator on her stockinged feet. She pulls Tupperware containers from the fridge and spins them onto the counter like Frisbees. "I'm afraid it's leftovers." She snaps the lids off one by one. "Wash your hands and then set the table."

We both sit there, frozen, not wanting to tell her what happened to Freddie.

Mom crashes around the kitchen. She grabs spoons and dishes, then dollops mounds of veggie stew and some slimy green stuff onto plates. She slings them into the microwave, wipes her hands on a kitchen towel, and then spins around like a whirling dervish.

"What's wrong with you?" She dashes over to the table and puts her hand on Crispy's forehead. "Are you sick?" Her eyes get wide.

"Freddie," Crispy whines. "I want Freddie."

"Where's Freddie? Has something happened to him?" She glances around the kitchen. "I *knew* something was missing."

She turns to me. "Kassandra Urania O'Roarke, what's going on?"

I cringe, both from her use of my full name and from her assumption that whatever is wrong must be my fault.

"We lost Freddie." I bite my lip and stare into my lap.

"What?" She plops down into the chair next to Crispy. "What do you mean 'you lost him'? Where? How?"

Crispy whimpers something about the cemetery, then starts blubbering. He can't get another word out.

"We were following the clue from the riddle," I jump in. "Remember, the tombstone?" My brain is scrambling to come up with the best way to tell this story.

"The cemetery across the woods? I thought you were at the bakery." Mom scrunches her eyebrows.

"We were looking for the tombstone."

"Your scavenger hunt took you to the cemetery?" Mom squints at me. "I'm confused."

I nod my head. "Right. Anyway, Slug threw a dog biscuit—"

"Slug?"

"His real name is James. He's an orphan. His foster family—"

"How old is James, and where did you meet him?" Mom crosses her arms. She might as well shine a blinding light in my eyes and scratch her fingernails across a chalkboard. "Why would you go to the cemetery with someone you don't know? And how did you get there?" Her rapid-fire questions make her sound like some cop on TV.

"We were at Mrs. Patel's. James is a new boy, a friend of Butler's." Okay, maybe that's stretching the truth . . . but Butler *did* say he liked Slug's skateboard. "Oliver was driving us home and we stopped off at the cemetery to see if we could find the headstone, the one from the riddle. Slug—er, James—threw the biscuit as a joke. And you know how much Freddie loves dog biscuits." I talk as fast as I can without taking a breath, trying to get it all out before Mom can interrupt with more questions.

"Freddie ran into the forest." Crispy sobs some more. "He's going to get eaten by a wolf." He wipes his nose on his sleeve.

Mom puts her arm around his shoulders and pulls him in for a hug. "Ferrets are very resourceful creatures. Everything will be okay." She glances over at me with worry in her eyes. I can tell she's afraid everything *won't* be okay.

I pull the last tissue from my spy vest and offer it to Crispy. I wish there was something I could do to get Freddie

back. Watching my little brother fall apart is making my stomach upset.

"Why don't I call Animal Control—"

"No!" Crispy and I shout in unison.

"We can't let Agent Killjoy find Freddie." I remember Stinkerton's twitching mustache and bad breath when he came to the door the other day. He threatened to close down the petting zoo if another animal escaped. Of course, Freddie is a pet and not really part of the zoo, but that wouldn't matter to Stinky Pinky.

"Maybe someone already found him. I've got to call." Mom slips her phone out of the back pocket of her scrubs.

"Wait!" I jump up from the table. "I forgot to tell you. Agent Pinkerton came to the house. He threatened to shut down the petting zoo."

Mom gives me the side-eye. "Pinky was here?" Pinky is her pet name for Agent Stinkerton. I think it's hilarious.

"A neighbor might have seen Chewbacca in their garden." I cringe. I should have told Mom earlier. But I didn't want to worry her . . . and I wanted to investigate the comings and goings of our chimp.

"What? That's impossible. Chewy is in her pen." Mom looks from me to Crispy. "Isn't she?"

I nod, hoping it's true.

"First things first. We find Freddie." Mom must have Animal Control on speed dial, because a second later she's asking if anyone's turned in a ferret. Mom shakes her head. *Nope.*

She's talking for way too long. I hope she's not talking to Stinkerton. "Pinky says he'll be on the lookout for Freddie."

Yeah, I bet he will—so he can close us down!

Crispy gives me a worried look. We've got to find Freddie before Killjoy does.

It occurs to me, maybe Stinkerton Killjoy is the petnapper. He definitely has the means. And he's just evil enough to do something like steal pets for rewards. Maybe I should be investigating "Pinky."

"Come on. Let's have dinner. Then we'll figure out what to do about Freddie." Mom pulls our plates out of the microwave. "Kassy, please set the table."

I get the place mats out of the drawer and set them on the table in our usual spots, with Mom in the middle. I fold three paper napkins and place them on the right-hand corner of the mats. Then I grab spoons and forks and set them neatly on top of the napkins. Maybe if I'm helpful and do everything right, Mom won't be angry.

Mom serves the hot plates heaping with food that looks like someone already ate it. She grabs a bag of kale chips and rips it open, as if that will somehow make the meal more appealing. I pour three glasses of orange juice—the best part of the dinner—and carefully squeeze them between my palms, barely getting them to the table without spilling.

I push my food around the plate with my fork, separating the green stuff from the brown-orange mushy stuff. Mom shoots me a look that lets me know I'd better get to eating and quit messing around. My stomach is twisted in fear for Freddie . . . but I don't want to bring it up. Crispy is upset enough. So, I hold my breath and swallow the first bite. It's just as yucky tonight as it was last night. *Oh well. Best to get it over with.* I pretend I'm eating one of Mrs. Patel's curries.

Crispy usually gobbles up Mom's cooking, but tonight he just hangs his head and stares down at his plate.

Mom lets us off easy and doesn't make us clean our plates. After we wash the dishes, she takes us to the clinic to use her office computer. We need to put up notices about Freddie online. Mom uploads his picture, and I type in a description: *Lost ferret. Brown with a white muzzle, black mask, and pink nose. Answers to "Freddie," loves dog biscuits, and has a problem with flatulence.*

"Maybe remove that part about the farting," Mom laughs. She's trying to cheer us up. But I can tell she's just as worried as we are.

"We need to offer a reward," Crispy says, leaning over the desk to point at the screen.

"Okay. Offer a fifty-dollar reward," Mom says.

"Freddie's worth more than fifty dollars!" Crispy jumps up and down.

"Freddie is priceless." Mom tries to sound upbeat as she pushes send on our message to the neighborhood list. "The reward is just frosting on the cake."

"We need to make flyers and post them everywhere." Crispy points to the printer.

"Good idea." I copy and paste the picture and info into a new document, enlarge everything, and center it to make it look nice. "What do you think?"

Crispy pouts. "Why am I in the picture? What if they think I'm Freddie?"

I snort. "You may have beady eyes and love dog biscuits, but I don't think anyone will mistake you for a ferret . . . a rodent, maybe."

"Freddie isn't a rodent!" Crispy's white muzzle turns red.

"Right, *you're* the rodent."

"Calm down, you two." Mom ruffles my hair, and I flinch. I hate it when she does that.

But teasing my brother calms me down. It makes everything seem more bearable, more normal, as if someone really might find a little ferret lost in the forest. I print out twenty fliers.

"Let's go post the flyers." I gather them up from the printer. They're warm, and the ink smell reminds me of the library.

"Not tonight." Mom takes the flyers from my hands. "We'll do it first thing in the morning, after you feed the animals and before I open the clinic."

"But Freddie can't—" I say and then stop myself from finishing the sentence. *survive in the woods on his own all night*

Mom shuts down the computer. "Come on you two." She leads us through the clinic door and back into the house. "We'll find Freddie in the morning. Don't worry. He'll be all right." The quiver in her voice tells me otherwise.

Crispy and I exchange a glance. The glint in his eyes says it all: he has other plans.

11

NOCTURNAL NAUGHTINESS

I JUST KNOW CRISPY IS UP TO SOMETHING. He does his barn chores before Mom even asks. He even scoops the poop out of all the pens. Since that's usually my job, I'm ecstatic—extra time to set up my booby trap.

Crispy's bedroom is on the first floor, next to Mom's and right below mine. If he's going to make a break for it tonight, it will have to be through his window—otherwise Mom will hear.

I poke my head into the barn to make sure he's still busy with chores. Then I run back into the house and check on Mom. She's doing some weird experiment in the kitchen involving mason jars, some sour-smelling fluid, and animal parts. *I don't even want to know . . .*

"I'm going to go wash up." I almost say *I'm going to go clean my room*, but I think better of it. Mom would know for sure something was up.

She just nods and drops something yucky into a jar.

Up in my room, I pull my toolbox out from under the bed and retrieve a ball of string and a pair of scissors. I unwind a good twenty feet of string and then attach a bell to one end. I fasten that end to a tack, which I push into the wall just below my windowsill. At the other end of the string, I attach a heavy pencil with a sturdy eraser. Carefully pushing the corner of the window screen open a crack, I stuff the pencil through. I slowly let out more and more string until the pencil is dangling just outside Crispy's bedroom window.

I dash back downstairs, turn on the faucet in the bathroom, and shut the door on my way out. Mom will think I'm in there. Glancing both ways down the hall, I tiptoe into Crispy's bedroom, sprint to the window, and tug on the frame. *Chicken-fried steak!* It's stuck. The pencil waves at me from the other side of the glass.

In the distance, I see Crispy crossing the lawn, carrying Poseidon's slop bucket. I yank at the window casing. It doesn't budge. I glance around the bedroom, looking for something I could use to tap on the window frame and loosen it.

Crispy's bed is heaped with a whole zoo of stuffed animals. Not your usual cute and cuddly kind, either, but aardvarks and lizards. His wall is covered with *Star Wars* posters. On his book shelf, there's a peanut butter sandwich crust, the complete set of Harry Potter books, Legos . . . and a worm farm.

Mesmerized by the worms burrowing into the earth, I bend over to take a closer look.

There's another universe inside that aquarium, an entire world run by worms. I'm not a big fan of worms, myself. But at least they don't have wings. *Are we like worms to some other bigger beings?* Maybe someone is looking down at us thinking they're glad we can't fly.

Not finding any tools, I settle for one of Crispy's hiking boots. I tap the heel against the window frame. Nothing. I tap harder, but it still won't budge. I bang the boot against the frame. *Bam!* That thud loosens the frame, all right, and makes a big black mark on the wood—probably alerting Mom to what she calls my "shenanigans." But I can't stop now.

Crispy is almost back to the house. Concentrating on his mission, he doesn't see me lurking inside his room. I open the window and poke my finger through the corner of the screen, then push until my whole hand is outside. *Brussels sprouts!* The pencil is just out of my reach.

I pull a chair over to the window, kneel on it, and stick my whole arm outside. My fingertips graze the pencil. It swings away. I hold my breath and wait for it to arc back toward the window. *Bingo!* I pull it inside, untie the pencil, and knot the string to the window handle. If Crispy opens his window, the tension on the string will ring the bell. I shut the window, put the chair back in its place, throw the boot back into the closet, and make my escape. Hopefully, Crispy won't notice . . . Eventually, Mom will. But I'll have to deal with that later.

I'm about to pop back into the bathroom when Mom appears out of nowhere. "What's all that racket?"

I blink at her like a deer in the headlights.

"Why is the water running?"

I hold up the pencil. "I forgot my pencil in the living room, so I ran down to get it and tripped and fell . . . ?" My fib sounds more like a question than a statement.

"You fell down the stairs?" Mom rushes to my side. "Petunia, are you okay?"

I nod.

"No more running on the stairs."

"Right."

"And the water?"

"I remembered the pencil when I was washing up."

Mom narrows her eyes. "Turn off the faucet and get ready for bed. And next time, shut it off before you leave the bathroom."

"Right." I slip into the bathroom, turn off the tap, and then head back upstairs to my attic, avoiding Mom's prying eyes as I pass her in the hallway.

At the top of the stairs, I stop and listen. Crispy and Mom are talking on the landing below. He brushes his teeth and washes up for bed without being asked. He even kisses Mom goodnight.

Now I'm certain Crispy is up to something. He must be planning to look for Freddie. And if he does, I'm going with him. I can't let him search that dark, scary forest all alone. Mom would *want* me to go with him. Well, Mom probably wouldn't want either of us going out after dark, but if Crispy goes, I'm going with him. We've got to find Freddie before he gets . . . I don't even want to think about it.

I lay in bed reading the dictionary on high alert. I'm wearing my jeans and flannel shirt under my nightgown. If Crispy opens his window, the bell on my end of the string will tinkle. I can hardly keep my eyes open. But I don't want to fall asleep in case Crispy escapes.

Reading the dictionary isn't helping me stay awake. I crawl out of bed and grab my spy vest. Maybe Lyncoya's diary will keep my interest. I slip the diary out of my vest pocket and climb back into bed.

I flip to the page with the riddles. I still haven't solved the third one: *It's seen in the middle of March and April but can't be seen at the beginning or end of either month.* March and April—that's springtime. You can see trees bloom and robins show up. But those can be seen at the beginning and end of both months, too. Sometimes Tennessee gets freak ice storms in March . . . but never in April. *Hmmm.*

I lay the diary on the bed and rub my eyes. Maybe I was wrong. Maybe Crispy *is* just sleeping. I roll over and turn off my light. I feel my breathing getting heavier. I drift off to sleep.

In my dream, a mother cow is trying to use her big teeth to attach a tiny cowbell around her calf's neck. The calf is mooing. *Fried catfish!* The ringing bell isn't just in my dream. Crispy is on the move!

I jump out of bed, stuff my feet into my sneakers, and fly down the stairs as quietly as possible. I hightail it out the front door and dash across the lawn, toward Crispy at the corral. *Wait . . . what's he doing?* In the beam of the floodlight, I see him pull a carrot from his pocket, open the corral, and lure Spittoon out the gate. The camel is only too happy to follow.

I step forward into the light. "What do you think you're doing?" I whisper, bending over and putting my hands on my knees to catch my breath. Even though it's still warm out, the wind is picking up, and the breeze is cool on my face.

Crispy jumps. The little dork is wearing his bright blue Star Wars pajamas. "Geez, Kas. You scared me." He shines his flashlight at my face.

I squint and cover my eyes. "Where are you taking Spittoon?"

"He's going to help me track down Freddie." Crispy pets the camel's nose. True, Spittoon is allergic to cats—he has a sneezing fit anytime he's near cat hair. But I don't think his sneeze alarm works with ferrets.

Spittoon kneels down. Crispy climbs on his back, just in front of his hump, and holds onto a tuft of hair. Once Crispy's aboard, the camel lumbers to its feet. Crispy bends down and hands me his flashlight. "Shine this so we can see where we're going."

"Where are we going?"

"To the forest to find Freddie!"

I shine the light across the lawn. In the distance, trees dance in the wind like angry demons. "This is a bad idea," I say as we take off.

Up ahead, a shadowy figure runs across the lawn into the trees. I gasp. "What was that?"

Before Crispy can answer, Spittoon takes of running.

"Wait!" I yell.

Spittoon is running at full tilt. Crispy is bouncing around like a Ping-Pong ball. And the shadowy figure is shrieking at the top of its lungs. It lopes off into the woods. *Wait a second!*

That high-pitched scream is familiar . . . and so is the lopsided loping. *Chewy!* How'd she get out of the barn?

I take off running as fast as I can after Spittoon, chasing Chewy into the forest. "Chewy, come back! Spittoon, stop! Crispy, wait!" None of them listen to me.

Leaves rustle, branches snap, Spittoon snorts, and Chewy screams. I think of the cemetery on the other side of the woods. We're better off waking the dead than waking Mom—she'll ground us for life if she finds out about this "escapade," as she'd call it.

The flashlight isn't much good in the thick of the forest while I'm running at full speed. Branches scratch my arms, but I keep going. The bouncing flashlight beam only makes the path seem creepier.

"Wait up!" My chest hurts from running so fast. I can hardly breathe.

I wave the heavy flashlight above my head to keep the branches from whacking me in the face. Something grabs my hair. *That better not be a bat!* Terrified, I wield the flashlight as a weapon.

Flailing my arms around, I run straight into a tree. *Ouch!* My glasses fly off, and I hit the ground. If I lose my glasses, Mom will have a cow. I grope around for them on my hands and knees. They should make special glasses for detectives, glasses that stay on your head no matter what dangerous situation you encounter. Maybe I could get one of those elastic bands Ronny uses for soccer.

The ground is damp. Leaves stick to my palms as I crawl. Something sticky clings to my hand. I don't even want to know what it is. *Where are my glasses?*

The shrieking and pounding of hooves stop. I listen to the sounds of the night—crickets, the wind in the trees, and cars in the distance. *What happened to Crispy, Chewy, and Spittoon?*

My left knee comes down on something sharp, and I hear a snapping sound. *Oh no!* I reach back. Sure enough . . . my glasses. Snapped right in half. Luckily, I have medical tape in my spy vest.

I tuck the flashlight under my arm, pinning it to my side while I tape the two halves of my glasses together. I slide them onto my nose, stand up, and shine the light around the forest. No sign of any camels, chimps, or brothers.

My heart is racing. *Where are they?* I can't see them. I can't hear them. Maybe I can smell them. I sniff the moist night air. If Freddie's nearby, I should be able to get a whiff of him! I close my eyes, breathing in the sour, spicy smell of wet leaves and pine needles. A hint of musky animal wafts on the breeze.

"Crispy? Where are you?" I shout into the darkness. All I hear is the echo of my own voice.

I point the flashlight up the path and head deeper into the forest. An owl hoots, and the hairs on my arms stand up. It's one thing to be in the woods during the day, when everything is bright and buzzing. But at night, when nocturnal creatures crawl out of their holes and cracks . . . it's different.

Up ahead, a rustling sound stops me in my tracks. I listen on the wind to determine where its coming from. A dog's bark ricochets off the trees. I take off running in its direction. The barking gets louder as I jog down a narrow path toward the cemetery. Up ahead, I see the outline of a shack and, in front of it, Spittoon's lumpy silhouette.

"Crispy!" I pick up my pace. It's not easy to run down a narrow path in the dark. Branches whack me in the face. Roots try to trip me and throw me to the ground. And something keeps swooping at my hair. *Please not bats. Please not bats. Please not bats.* I jog to the beat of the chant in my head.

Spittoon is munching on the leaves of a poplar tree. A commotion inside the shack makes him stop, tilt his head, and spit.

I shine the light on the door to the dilapidated shed. It's open a crack. Slowly, I reach out into the darkness to open the door. *Ack!* Something touches my hand and I jump back.

12

FINDING HAIRY PAWTER

THE DOOR TO THE SHACK SWINGS OPEN. "Kassy. Look!" My brother is petting the noggin of a very hairy dog. I shine the flashlight on the animal. *What!* It's Hairy Pawter, Mr. Swindell's cockapoo. *What's he doing here?*

"You found Hairy Pawter!"

"Chewy found him." Crispy points at the chimp.

Chewy is sitting on the wooden floor next to Crispy, grooming the dog, pretending to pick fleas from its fur and eat them . . . or maybe she's not pretending. *Has she been licking him, too? Gross!* Other than Hairy and Chewy, the shack is empty except for cobwebs and a couple of dusty old shelves.

This shack used to be on our property before Mom sold

the horse ranch. Dad used it to store stuff. Now it just stores spiders and bats and other creepy crawlies.

"Spittoon followed Chewy here to this old shed, and Hairy Pawter was inside."

"Was the door open or closed when you got here?"

Crispy looks at Spittoon like he's expecting the camel to answer. "I don't remember. I just heard barking—"

"Did you have to open the door or not?"

Crispy wrinkles his brows. "I guess so. It all happened so fast."

I shine the light around and see a bowl on the floor. "Why is there a bowl of dog food?" Unless Hairy Pawter travels with his own kibble, someone hid him here.

"We better get home before Mom finds out we're gone, or we'll be grounded for life." I look around for a collar or leash, then remember I already handed them over to Mr. Swindell. *Drat!* I search the pockets of my vest. I do have Hairy Pawter's bandana . . . and my usual string and scissors. I tie the bandana around his furry neck and cut a length of string. Then I fasten the string to the bandana. *It'll have to do.*

"Come on." I gently tug on the string. Hairy wags his tail wildly and sniffs my shoes.

"But what about Freddie?"

What about Freddie, indeed. I shine the light all around the inside of the shed just in case Freddie's hiding someplace. He does like to crawl into small cracks. "Freddie, are you here?"

The stale air smells like wet dog, not musky ferret. "Do you think if Freddie were here there'd be any food left?" I point to the dog dish.

"Maybe he's scared to come out." Crispy waves away some cobwebs and explores the corners of the shed. "Here, boy. Come out, Freddie. It's me, Percy."

Maybe Crispy is right. Freddie loves dog food almost as much as dog biscuits, but he isn't crazy about dogs. If he *is* locked up in this nasty shack, he might be hiding. He could be peeking his little black nose out of some tiny hole watching us and we'd never know it.

"He's not here." I head out the door with Hairy Pawter in tow.

"How do you know?"

"I just do." I don't want to upset Crispy by mentioning Freddie's odor.

"I'm not leaving without Freddie."

"We have to get Hairy Pawter home. And *we* have to get home." I start down the path, hoping Crispy will follow. "We'll find Freddie. Don't worry. Leave the door open, and then if Freddie gets hungry, he'll find the dog food."

I glance back hoping my brother will be persuaded by logic. And it seems he is.

Chewy is sitting up on Spittoon's hump, and Crispy is pulling on the camel's lead rope. I tug on Hairy Pawter's string, and together we stumble through the woods toward the house. I hope Mom didn't notice we were gone . . . otherwise, we'll be spending the rest of the summer on house arrest.

I let out a huge sigh of relief when we exit the woods and make it back onto the lawn. Chewy leaps off the camel and takes my free hand. Crispy leads Spittoon to his corral and lures him inside with another carrot. I take Chewy back inside the barn and give her a banana, which she happily carries into her enclosure. While she's busy munching, I examine the lock on her pen.

I'm guessing she's been making nightly trips out to that shed. That must be where she got Hairy Pawter's collar and leash. Maybe that's where she got the cat, too. *How has she been escaping?*

Hairy Pawter licks my hand while I fiddle with the lock. It looks normal. The wheels in my brain are whirring. I bet our dognapper lured Hairy Pawter to the shed with food and then planned to collect the reward from poor, distraught Mr. Swindell.

Mr. Swindell is probably worried sick. I should tell him I found Hairy. But I can't do that without telling Mom . . . and, whatever happens, I'm not going to risk being grounded for life.

I have a plan. I prepare a bowl of kibble and set it inside Chewy's pen. I open the gate and, for good measure, throw a couple of dog biscuits inside. Hairy Pawter runs in after them. I lock the gate behind him. I still have to figure out how Chewy is escaping. *Is she a lockpicker?* Chimps are pretty smart. And they do use tools.

Maybe now that she has a friend for a sleepover, she'll stay put. It will be a little weird explaining the cockapoo in her pen to Mom. But Chewy *did* have a kitten in there earlier. Maybe I should employ Chewy as my assistant. She has a knack for finding lost pets. And I could pay her peanuts. Adults complain about getting paid peanuts. But Chewbacca wouldn't mind.

I meet Crispy outside the corral. We might as well face whatever awaits us in the house together. From here, everything looks the same as when we left. The house is dark except the porch light, and that's always on.

I creep across the lawn, and Crispy follows. I left the flashlight in the barn, but even if I had it, I wouldn't turn it on. We're trying to be invisible.

Crispy's humming to himself. I turn around and put my finger to my lips. His eyes get wide, like he's seen a T. rex on our porch or a spaceship in our front yard. I whirl around.

Garlic cheese grits! Mom is barreling toward us in her bathrobe and slippers, sparks flying from her eyes. She must really be mad. Without a word, she grabs me by the elbow, then Crispy, and drags us into the house.

"It's Percy's fault," I explain. "He—"

Mom shakes her head and makes a strange growling sound. I shut up.

"But we found—" Crispy tries.

"Shhh." Mom leads Crispy to his bedroom and points to his bed. Then she leads me upstairs to my bedroom.

"Kassandra, I'm disappointed in you." She has a sad look in her bloodshot eyes.

"I can explain—"

"It's late. I have to get up for surgery in the morning. Your explanation will have to wait." She points at my bed. "Get in bed and don't get out again until the sun's up."

I nod and start to crawl in.

Mom sighs. "Take off those filthy clothes first," she mutters as she leaves.

I'd better come up with an explanation before dawn. I don't think Mom will be sympathetic to my story about booby-trapping Crispy's window, especially if she sees I broke the screen. Then again, she should be happy I'm watching out for him . . . On the other hand, I should have told her when I heard him leave the house . . . Then again, we did find Mr. Swindell's dog. That counts for something.

We also discovered that Chewy is escaping her pen at night. That's huge. I mean, what if she went out and tipped over trash cans or ruined the neighbors' gardens?

What if Chewy had gotten hurt? Maybe we saved her life. Or maybe we stopped Agent Killjoy from capturing her. He'd shut down Lemontree Petting Zoo in a second. Then where would we be? Mom would have to get rid of all the animals, and Crispy would lose all his friends . . . and probably his mind.

So really, I saved Chewy and Crispy and the petting zoo. *Mom should thank me.*

I'm too excited to go to sleep. I change into my nightgown, brush some leaves out of my hair, and crawl into bed. I read Lyncoya's diary by the light of my backup flashlight. I wonder if he walked through that same forest, under those same trees. Some of them might have been saplings then. Or maybe they already towered over him and their branches slapped his face as he ran down that same game trail. Maybe he snuck out of his house some night, looking for a lost friend.

I close my eyes and hope I dream of Lyncoya and his secrets.

13

CAT-CAKES

THE NEXT MORNING, I GET UP EARLY to do my chores. Maybe if I clean out the barn and organize the food storage closet, Mom will be lenient. I check on Chewy to make sure she hasn't flown the coop again. Hairy Pawter greets me with his goofy grin and waving tail. I pat him on the head through the bars, then throw him a couple of dog biscuits. *Wait until Mom sees Chewy's new friend!*

I bide my time doing extra chores. I'm afraid to go inside for breakfast. But hiding will probably just make it worse. With a deep breath, I march across the lawn to get it over with.

I quietly open the front door, slink into the kitchen, and slip onto a chair at the table, still trying to be invisible.

Mom smiles at me. "I'm making pancakes. Want to help?"

Hmmm . . . why is she being so nice? She knows pancakes are my favorite.

"Look!" Mom flips a pancake. "I made a cat."

Okay. Now I'm really worried. We haven't made animal-shaped pancakes since I was a little kid. With caution, I get up and approach the griddle.

"What were you and Percy doing in the woods last night?" Mom asks like it's no big deal, like she's asking "How was school?" or "What do you want on your pancakes?"

"Percy went out to look for Freddie." I glance up to get a read on her face. "You know how much he loves that ferret." I scoop up some batter in a big spoon and drip it onto the griddle. It's *supposed* to be a Mickey Mouse shape, but the batter spreads out into three blobs. It looks more like a mutant cactus.

"That's what I figured." Mom scrapes her cat off the griddle and slides it onto a plate. "Here, eat it while it's hot."

What is she up to? I take the plate and head to the table.

"I'm making a ferret for Percy." With the steady hand of a skilled veterinarian, Mom performs the intricate operation of forming a ferret out of pancake batter.

"Where is Percy?" Usually he's up before me. I slather butter on my pancakes and then douse them in maple syrup. Mom has already poured me a big glass of orange juice. In fact, she's set the table with three glasses of OJ, Crispy's favorite Star Wars napkins, and every kind of syrup and jam we have.

"Wasn't he with you in the barn?" Mom flips another flapjack. "I have good news for him," she smiles.

I shake my head. *Yum.* These pancakes are tasty. I take another big bite. Doing chores always makes me hungry. "He must be sleeping in after our . . . " I stop myself from saying "nocturnal adventure." Mom and I look at each other.

Crispy never sleeps in.

The last bite of cat-cake claws at my stomach. *Oh no.*

Mom drops the spatula and dashes out of the kitchen. I leap up to follow her. We race to Crispy's bedroom. She throws the door open. Empty. The cat-cake in my stomach must have had a hairball, because I feel sick.

"Percy!" Mom calls. "Perseus!" She's on the move. Passing the empty bathroom, she wipes her hands on her apron, yanks it off, and throws it on a side table in the hallway. "Go see if your brother is in the barn."

In a few seconds, I'm screaming across the lawn at top speed before skidding to a stop in front of the corral. My heart sinks. Sure enough, Spittoon is gone.

I climb over the fence and survey the pasture to make sure he isn't just hiding behind the barn. But there's no sign of the camel . . . or the brother.

For good measure, I check inside the barn. The animals are all munching on their breakfasts. Hairy Pawter barks when he sees me.

"Have any of you seen Crispy?" I ask as I pace up and down, checking all the enclosures. I stop in front of Apollo's pen. "Do you know where he is?"

The cougar cub looks up at me and yawns. Crispy is always telling me the clever things Apollo says. I guess the cub is more of a philosopher than a detective.

Cheese and rice! I'm starting to think like Crispy. But it makes sense—if anyone knows where my brother is, it would be his animal friends. *His only friends.*

I sprint back to the house. *Brussels sprouts!* Mom's on the phone with Dad. She shoots me a questioning look.

I shake my head. But I'm betting he went back to that old shack.

"You've got to find him." Mom sounds desperate. "I have surgery in half an hour. I can't—"

I hold my breath and listen to the one-sided conversation. I wish I could hear what Dad is saying.

"Okay. Thanks. See you soon." Mom hangs up the phone. "Call the bakery and see if he's there. I have to open the clinic."

I nod and slide across the linoleum floor to the phone. (Yeah, It's attached to the wall. Our ranch house is *that* old.)

I punch in the number by heart.

"Patel Pastries." I recognize Butler's voice.

"Have you seen my brother?"

"Carrot?"

I roll my eyes. "It's *Kassy*. Have you seen Crispy?"

"No. Why?"

"He took off on Spittoon."

"The camel?"

"Who else do you know named Spittoon?"

"Why would he run away?"

"He went out looking for Freddie."

"I'll keep an eye out. A boy on a camel shouldn't be hard to miss."

"Thanks." I hang up. *Should I go back out and look in the woods? Or should I wait for Dad?*

In a missing person case, every minute matters. I check the pockets of my spy vest for supplies. I need to replenish my emergency granola bar supply, refill my water bottle, and get my miniature flashlight from under my pillow. I put on my fedora and dash outside. I want to go look for Crispy on my own, but unless I want to be grounded for life, I decide to wait for Dad.

When Dad finally pulls into the driveway, I've been pacing back and forth on the front porch for fifteen minutes. As soon as the car stops, Ronny jumps out. She drop-kicks her soccer ball, and it boomerangs off the porch railing. She's a crack shot.

"Have you found your brother yet?" Dad's wearing a navy blue suit. He must have been on his way to work when Mom called. He's a lawyer, which might come in handy if we have to bail Crispy out of jail.

"I bet he's in the woods looking for Freddie."

"Let's form a search party." Dad strides across the lawn.

I follow him, and Ronny skips to keep up.

"He took Spittoon." I'm walking as fast as I can.

"Why'd he do that?" Dad shakes his head.

"He thinks Spittoon can track Freddie." Talking as fast as I can, I explain how we lost Freddie and found Hairy Pawter in the old shack, and why Crispy might think Freddie would go back there for food. I can tell Dad is only half listening.

"Your mother says someone emailed that they found Freddie. They're coming by later this morning to return him and collect the reward." Dad enters the woods on the same path we used last night. He knows every inch of this place.

"Really? Someone found Freddie?" That explains Mom's good mood. *Why didn't she tell me?*

"Maybe we should offer a reward for Percy." Ronny spins the soccer ball on her finger.

"The reward," I whisper. Whoever turns up to collect the reward might just be the dognapper—or, in this case, ferret-napper. I've got to stake out the clinic and see who it is. *Brussels sprouts!* That reminds me. Hairy Pawter's still locked up in Chewy's pen. I've got to return him to Mr. Swindell.

"Look, it's Spittoon." Dad points. "Who's that with him?"

I look up. "Hey, it's Slug." He's leading Spittoon. *But where's Crispy?*

Dad shakes his head. "Who names their kid Slug?"

Ronny laughs. "Slugs are slimy and disgusting. And if you put salt on them, they dissolve."

"Now *that's* disgusting!" I run ahead.

"Is this your camel?" Slug asks with a smirk.

"Where did you find him?" I take ahold of the lead rope.

"By that old abandoned shed." Slug points to the shack.

"Have you seen my brother? He's missing."

"Nope. Sorry. Only the camel." Slug smiles. "Hey, good news about Freddie at least."

"Yeah."

Dad and Ronny catch up to us.

"This is my dad."

"Good to meet you, Mr. O'Roarke." Slug extends his hand and my dad shakes it. "I'm sorry to hear your son is missing. I'm sure he'll turn up." *Wow! Slug is really good with parents.* "Glad the ferret is back." He stuffs his hands into the pockets of his leather jacket. "See ya later, Kassy. Good luck finding your brother." He does an about-face and jogs back up the path.

"How do you know that kid?" Dad asks.

"I met him at the bakery. He's a friend of Butler's."

"You haven't mentioned him before."

"He's not *my* friend." I shrug. "Why would Crispy leave Spittoon?"

"Good question." Dad calls out for Percy some more.

"Maybe he's taking a nap." Ronny kicks her soccer ball straight through the trees. It hits the side of the shack. "What's in there, anyway?"

"Nothing but bad memories." Dad leads the way to the shack.

"Percy!" Dad shouts again.

"Percy!" Ronny joins in.

As we approach the shack, I glimpse a bright blue swatch beneath a tree. The cat-cakes start clawing at my stomach again. "Crispy!" I yell as I run toward the blue pajamas.

Crispy is lying motionless on the ground. His head is bleeding. "Dad!" I scream at the top of my lungs. "Percy is hurt. He's hurt bad."

14

MISSING CRISPY

AT THE HOSPITAL, I SIT QUIETLY READING Lyncoya's diary, waiting for Crispy to wake up. We're all waiting for him to wake up. Mom and Dad are in the corridor, talking to the doctor, and Ronny is sitting next to me on the plastic couch. She rocks back and forth, hugging her soccer ball.

Crispy looks so small lying in the hospital bed. There's a big white bandage around his head and tubes going into his arm. We've been here for hours already. The doctors say he might have a concussion.

I'm shivering. Crispy's hospital room is like a refrigerator. Ronny's wearing shorts—she must be freezing. I scoot closer to her until our legs are touching. She glances over at me with tears in her eyes.

My whole body feels numb. *He's got to be okay. He's just got to.* I bury myself in the diary to keep myself from crying.

It's my fault Crispy got hurt. *Why didn't I keep an eye on him?* I should have known he'd try again. I should have followed him.

I close the diary and slide it back into my spy vest. It's impossible to concentrate. I put my elbows on my knees and join Ronny in rocking back and forth.

Mom peeks her head through the curtain in front of the hospital room door. She quietly pulls the curtain aside. "Poor girls," she whispers. "You look cold." She disappears again.

I hear Dad's voice in the hallway. Then Mom reappears with a white flannel blanket. She wraps it around me and Ronny, and the warmth makes all of my muscles relax like I'm sinking into a hot bath.

"They keep them in a heating oven." Mom gently places a second flannel blanket over Crispy. When she scoots a heavy chair closer to the bed, his eyelids flicker. She stops and looks at him, then takes his hand in hers.

"Mom?" he whimpers and opens his eyes.

Crispy's alive! I'm so happy I jump up and kiss him.

"What happened?" he asks in a weak voice. "Where am I?"

"You hit your head on a tree branch. You're in the hospital. You'll be okay." She smiles down at him.

Mom's words take a huge weight off my heart. I hope she's not just saying it so he won't be scared. *I'm scared, too.*

Dad enters the room. "Hey, sport. How do you feel? Quite a bump on your head."

"Freddie?" Crispy moans. "I didn't find him."

"Didn't your mom tell you?" Dad looks at Mom.

"A girl returned him this morning while your dad was out looking for you." Mom pats his hand. "Freddie is fine. He's waiting for you at home."

Freddie! I had almost forgotten about him. "Who returned him? Did you give her the reward?"

"Of course I did." Mom glances over at me and then turns back to Crispy. "And I gave Freddie a peanut butter sandwich." She kisses his hand. "And put him in your bedroom. He's safe and sound and can't wait to see you."

"Who was the girl?" I take out my detective notebook. "What's her name?"

"It was Kelly." Mom tucks the covers under Crispy's arms. "Your friend from school."

"Kelly Finkelman?" I'd hardly call her my friend . . . more like my nemesis. I write her name in my notebook. *Could Kelly be the petnapper? Why would she steal pets for the reward money?* Maybe she needs new pom-poms. Whatever she's up to, I'm going to find out.

Mom stand up, bends over Crispy, and kisses him on the cheek. "One of us should take the girls home," she says to Dad.

"I'll do it. You stay here with Percy."

"Will you be okay on your own until I get home?" Mom asks me.

Duh. "I'm nearly thirteen."

"Check on the animals when you get home."

"I will."

"And don't leave the property!"

"I won't."

"The techs are still in the clinic if you need anything." Mom taps her phone and makes a call. "Caroline? Yeah, he's going to be fine. They're discharging him in the next couple of hours. Can you do me a favor and keep an eye on Kassy until we get home? Her father will be dropping her off soon. Thanks."

"I'll be fine, Mom." I throw the blanket off my legs. "I can take care of myself."

Mom gives me the side-eye. "Feed the animals and then go straight to the clinic and wait for Caroline to get off work. She'll stay with you until we get home."

"Caroline doesn't need to babysit me." *Does Mom think I'm a baby?*

"Come on, pumpkin. Let's get you home." Dad holds his arm out. "Ronny, you too."

"I want to stay here with Percy." With the soccer ball under her arm, Ronny approaches Crispy's hospital bed. "Are you okay?"

He nods. "Ouch! My head hurts."

Ronny gives my dad a pleading look. "Please . . ."

Dad sighs. He's bouncing his car key up and down in his hand. "You can see Percy tomorrow when he's back at home." He looks at Mom. "If his mother doesn't mind."

Mom nods.

"Come on." Dad beckons to us. "Let's go, slowpokes."

Ronny drags her feet. When we reach the door, she runs back inside. She sets her soccer ball in the bed next to Crispy. "Xavier will keep you company."

I giggle to myself. *Her soccer ball has a name?* She must really like Crispy to leave Xavier here. She never goes anywhere without it.

I've been home for half an hour, feeding the animals their dinner. They can tell something's up. They all love Crispy. Apollo glares at me instead of eating his raw meat. Poseidon grunts but doesn't touch her trough of veggie peels. Raider washes his paws but holds onto his apple slice, looking around. Waiting for Crispy.

It's weird to be home without Crispy. Usually he's like my shadow and I'm trying to get away from him. But now, I miss him.

I make my way from one pen to the next, feeding the animals and making sure they have enough water. And I have to call Mr. Swindell as soon as possible. I should have done it this morning, but I was too worried about Crispy.

I scoop out a big helping of dog chow and head for Chewbacca's pen. Yeah, I know—she's a chimp. But she likes dog chow, and Mom has confirmed it is a healthy option for chimp care. As I approach the enclosure, I get a sinking feeling. *Fried catfish!* The door is ajar, and the pen is empty. Flustered, I trip over my own feet and spill the dog chow all over the dirt floor. Chewy's escaped again.

With everything that happened today, I forgot to tell Mom about Chewbacca's new skill, opening her pen. Hairy and Chewy are both gone. That clever chimp must have closed the barn door behind her. All I can figure is she has some tool she's using to the pick the locks. *Opposable thumbs come in handy.*

I know Mom said not to leave the property, but I really have no choice. I have to find Chewbacca and Hairy Pawter.

And I'd better hurry because I really don't want to be out in those creepy woods after dark. I check my spy watch. It's already a quarter to seven, and the clinic closes at seven thirty.

I throw some hay in the corral for Spittoon and Morpheus, then head across the lawn toward the forest. I'm guessing Chewbacca led Hairy Pawter back to the dilapidated shack where she found him. Something is going on with that shack, and I'm going to find out what.

I can't see any signs of Chewy or Hairy in the grass, but once I get to the path, I start looking for tracks. The ground is damp from a light afternoon rain. Mud is a detective's friend. I squat down and examine several pawprints. Some of them look like handprints with long palms and short thumbs. Those are definitely chimp prints. Others have a kidney bean–shaped pad with four toes—dog prints. *I'm on their trail.*

All my senses are on high alert as I hike through the forest. *Ouch!* A sticker bush brushes against my bare leg. I rub at the stinging scratches as I walk. I don't have time to stop. I have to find Chewy and Hairy before dark . . . and more importantly, before Mom gets home.

When you really listen, there's a whole chorus of sounds in the woods: birds singing, chipmunks chattering, twigs snapping. Leaves rustles as squirrels jump from branch to branch. And the bellows of your own breathing go *in-out, in-out, in-out* like an accordion.

I'm panting by the time I reach the shack. The door is cracked open. Muddy footprints lead inside. The food dish is empty, and so is the shed. Chewbacca and Hairy must have stopped by for a snack. A tuft of coarse black hair attached to the doorframe confirms that Chewy was here. Maybe she was scratching her back against the door, waiting for Hairy to finish his dinner.

Cheese and rice! Examining the ground around the shed, I notice the same two sets of footprints continuing down the path toward the cemetery. *Where are those two going?*

The sun is low in the sky and the clouds are turning orange. I pat the pockets of my spy vest. *Drat!* I left my backup flashlight in the barn. I have to get home before sunset. There's no way I could navigate this path in the dark!

I check my spy watch. It's seven. Caroline gets off work in half an hour. I'd better be back home by then. I pick up my pace.

Ouch! A branch slaps me in the face and nearly knocks my glasses off. *Wait! Where did the tracks go?* I examine the path. No tracks. I turn around and retrace my steps.

Aha! At a fork in the path, I see the tracks—heading in another direction. This new path takes me up a hill. Stumbling over roots and whacking branches out of the way with my notebook, I climb toward the last of the sunlight. The path ends, and I step out onto a manicured lawn. *Whoa!*

Across the lawn, the haunted mansion, surrounded by a wrought iron fence, stands on top of a hill. Between me and the mansion, there's another smaller brick building.

Did Chewbacca take Hairy to the mansion? Now that I'm on the grass, I've lost their trail. I hike up to the first building. *Could this be another house?* When I get closer, I see it has a big wooden garage door. *Pretty fancy for a garage.* I tiptoe up to one of the windows and peek inside. *Yikes!* An explosion of loud barking makes me jump back. *What in the world?*

I peer through the window again. *Wait!* That's Hairy Pawter. He's barking his head off and jumping at the window. *Wow!* He's loud. I thought there must be a dozen dogs in there. *Fried okra!* Chewy's right behind him. And is that a black cat with emerald green eyes sitting on top of an antique carriage?

I run around the building. All the doors are shut. *How'd they get inside?*

Next to the big garage door, there's a smaller regular door. I jiggle the doorknob. *Drat!* It's locked. I knock, but that only agitates the critters.

Hairy Pawter barks even louder, and Chewbacca joins in, squealing at the top of her lungs. "Shhh. Be quiet!" They don't mind me. I glance around. The ruckus they're making should get someone's attention.

I bend down and try to lift the big garage door from its handles. No luck. It's locked, too. *Now what? Go to the haunted mansion and see if someone is home?* My stomach sinks. I guess that's my only choice.

"Don't worry. I'll be back," I say to the garage door. Then I take off running.

I jog across the grass toward the gigantic house. The grounds are so big I'm out of breath when I reach the fence. The gate is open, so I go through.

The house is dark. My chest feels like it's full of stinging bees. I creep up the walkway to the front porch. *What if this house really is haunted?* I swallow hard and ring the doorbell.

15

THE TOMBSTONE

NOTHING. I WAIT A FEW SECONDS and try the doorbell again. On my tiptoes, shielding my eyes with my hand, I peek through the tiny rectangular window in the front door. *Aaah!* A hairy beast stares back at me! I take off running as fast as I can. *Was that a giant dog or a bear?*

I run back down the hill, heart pounding. I slip on the wet grass and hit the ground with a thud. The hill is so steep, I'm sliding down, head first. Holding out my arms doesn't help. I can't stop myself. *Aah!*

I bounce to a stop against a long evergreen hedge. *Ouch!* I spit out a mouthful of grass.

Sitting up, slightly dizzy, I assess the damage. I have grass stains on my knees and down the front of my shirt.

Mom isn't going to like that. My elbows are skinned but not bleeding.

Once the dizziness stops, I stand up and look around. I'm at the bottom of the hill, on the opposite side from the garage and path entrance. *Holy haunted house!* On the other side of the hedge is a small graveyard. The headstones look old. Some of them are tipped sideways. Others are cracked or crumbling. The whole place is overgrown with weeds.

Whoa! Could the tombstone from Lyncoya's riddle be here? I push my way through the hedge. What's a few more scratches?

I bend down to examine the first headstone: BOLIVIA 1817–1846. That person lived for only twenty-nine years. The next one says LADY NASHVILLE. She lived for eighteen years. Another says EMILIE, and another BUSIRIS. None of them lived over thirty years.

My legs itch as I wade through the weeds. *Wait! There it is!* COURT. I fall to my knees in front of the headstone. The weeds poke my arms and legs, but I don't care. *I found it!* The writing on the stone is ornate. There's something familiar about the jagged design in the curve of the letter *R*.

Oh no! There's another headstone that reads COURT . . . and another. COURT II, COURT III. So many Courts.

"Hey. You there!" A booming voice startles me. "What do you think you're doing?"

A giant snarling dog is loping toward me.

I jump up and start running. My legs feel like rubber. My head is spinning. *Where is the opening to the path?* I'm sprinting along the edge of the forest. *Where is it?* The dog is gaining on me. *Fried catfish! I'm a goner.*

I dive into the trees. Flailing my arms to keep the bushes from whacking me face, I run in what I hope is the direction of my house. *Thud!* I trip over a tree root and do a face-plant. *Ouch!* I bury my face in my arms and wait to be eaten by the beast.

My spy watch ticks off the seconds. *Tick. Tick. Tick.* I squeeze my eyes shut and hold my breath. I hear crickets singing, birds chirping, and the breeze blowing through the treetops . . . but no beast crashing through the woods.

I open one eye, then the other. Slowly, I raise my head and stare through the branches into the distance. The dim light and thick trees make it hard to see anything. Lifting myself to my hands and knees, I glance around. So far, no beast. Carefully, I stand up. Still no beast. Now if only I could find the path.

I'm pretending I'm not lost in the woods . . . at night . . . with a ferocious beast chasing me. *Concentrate, Kassy!* Okay, the dim light from the clearing is behind me. I just have to calm down and look for the glow of our farm. The floodlight should have kicked on at dusk.

Fumbling through the underbrush, I spot a tiny clearing up ahead. *Hooray!* I've found the path. But I'm all turned around. Luckily, my spy watch doubles as a compass. I learned how to use it last year in Girl Scouts.

Let's see. Our house is on the north side of Lemontree Heights. The cemetery, forest, and mansion are between our house and Main Street in downtown Lemontree Heights. Since I've just come from the mansion and I'm in the forest, I need to head north to get back to our house.

Luckily, the hands on my watch glow in the dark. Using the compass as my guide, I head north.

The night air is heavy and damp against my skin. The sounds of the forest, so pretty during the day, are spooky in the dark—hooting owls, fluttering bat wings, and screeching insects.

My pulse is racing. I hate to admit it, but I'm scared out of my wits. If I make it out of this alive, I swear I'll never leave the property again. I don't even care if Mom grounds me for life. *Please. I just have to get home.* I'm getting an itchy feeling in the corners of my eyes like I might start crying. I bite my lip and will myself to stop.

Come on, Kassy. Pull yourself together! Think of a nice cup of hot cocoa with marshmallows—tiny multicolored marshmallows and a double scoop of cocoa . . . with real milk . . . in your favorite Hello Kitty mug.

I didn't realize it, but I'm humming the "Bare Necessities" song from *The Jungle Book*. I sing as loud as I can to scare off the creatures of the night. And it works! Singing makes me less scared.

When I see the light at the end of the path, I shout with happiness. I pick up my pace. *Closer. Closer.* When I finally step onto the grass at the edge of our property, I pump my fist in the air. *Yes! I survived!*

Now I just have to survive the scolding I'll get from Mom . . . and convince her to take me back to that garage to free Chewy and Hairy. I can worry about the tombstones later.

Wait! Mom's car isn't here. Is she still at the hospital with Crispy? I hope he isn't worse. *Fried dill pickles!* Caroline's little red car is still parked in front of the vet clinic. She's probably been wondering where I am. What if she called Mom? I take a deep breath and prepare to do some desperate explaining.

I slink past the porch and around the side of the house to Crispy's bedroom window. I'm hoping it's still unlocked from his little adventure last night. On tiptoes, I steal through the flowerbed. Glancing around to make sure no one sees me, I push on the window frame. It squeaks and I stop. I take another deep breath and apply pressure to the frame as slowly and gently as possible.

Little by little, the window gives. When it's as high as I can push it, I hoist myself up onto the ledge and flop inside. *Thud!* I land on Crispy's floor. And there goes the rest of the screen. Mom definitely isn't going to be happy.

I hear footsteps coming down the hall. Quickly, I take the stack of books from Crispy's nightstand and spread them across the floor. Then, I jump into Crispy's bed and pull the covers up over my clothes.

"Kassy?" I hear Caroline's voice.

"In here," I say in my best imitation of a sleepy voice. I smell musk and then feel little feet walking on my legs. I peek out from under the covers. It's Freddie. I snatch him up and stuff him under the sheets with me.

"I've been looking for you." Caroline looks at me over the top of her little round glasses. *Yikes!* That reminds me . . . I bury my head in the pillow and slip off the elastic holding my glasses on my head.

"I've been napping." I fake a yawn and rub my eyes. "I was so tired when I got home from the hospital." Freddie pokes his nose out from under the sheets.

"What was that noise?" Caroline pushes her glasses up on her pointy nose.

"I must have pushed Crisp—ah, *my* books off the night-stand in my sleep." I point to the books spread across the floor.

Caroline bends down, picks up the books, and stacks them neatly on the nightstand. "Who's your favorite *Star Wars* character?"

"Hope Solo." *Why is she asking me about* Star Wars? I follow her gaze to the wall above my head. *Ah, right . . .* Crispy's walls are plastered with *Star Wars* posters.

"Isn't she a soccer player?" She sits down on the end of the bed.

Oops. "I mean Han Solo." I tug the covers up to my chin so she won't see I'm wearing my spy vest and all my clothes.

"What's that?" She points at the worm farm.

"A worm farm."

"You like worms?"

I nod.

"Like mother, like daughter," she laughs. "Your mom called. They're on their way home."

"Hello," Mom calls from the other room. "Kassy?" *Speak of the deviled egg.*

"We're in Kassy's bedroom," Caroline shouts.

I cringe.

Crispy is the first one through the bedroom door. He's got little strips of white tape above his right eyebrow and Ronny's soccer ball under his arm. "Hey! What are you doing in my bed?"

Caroline gives me a weird look. "This isn't your room?"

"I missed my brother." I hug his pillow. "So I wanted to be in his room." It's partially true—I did miss him.

Freddie licks Crispy's round pink face, and Crispy licks Freddie's little black nose. I cover my eyes so I don't have to watch their sloppy reunion.

Mom steps into the room and stares at me. "Kassandra, what have you been up to?" She stands over the bed. "Why are you in Percy's bed?" She reaches for my head. "And why in the world do you have twigs in your hair?"

My hand flies to my head. "What twigs?"

16

A GAGGLE OF GEESE

I GET UP BEFORE DAWN THE NEXT MORNING to do my chores and feed the animals before Mom notices Chewbacca is missing. I think I've figured out a way to get Chewy and Hairy Pawter back from the haunted mansion. I just need Ronny, Xavier, and some Girl Scout cookies.

I take the stairs two at time. The whirling sound of the dishwasher coming from the kitchen stops me in my tracks. *Brussels sprouts! Is Mom up already?* I've got to stop her from going to the petting zoo.

When I round the corner, Mom is putting on her rubber boots. *Oh no!*

"What are you doing up so early?" she asks.

"Just trying to help." I consider telling Mom about Chewy and Hairy and the garage and my suspicions about the petnapper . . . But she has a whole day of surgeries ahead. And she has a lot on her mind, especially since Crispy's accident. Anyway, I'm a pet detective—I'm supposed to be able to find pets and return them. And that's just what I'm going to do.

Mom scrunches her eyebrows. "Make yourself some breakfast. I'm going to the barn."

"No!" I slide across the floor on my stockinged feet and skid to a stop in front of her. "I'll go. You rest. Or prepare for your surgeries."

"Okay, what's going on?" She gives me the side-eye.

"Nothing." I shrug. "You need to get ready for work, so I'll take care of the animals."

"Tell you what." Mom's boots squeak as she walks over to the refrigerator. "Let's have some OJ, and then we'll go together." She pours two glasses of juice.

I wince. "Okay."

"Get your boots on." She sets a glass of juice on the table in front of me.

I jam my feet into my rubber boots. I sip the juice as slowly as possible to prolong the calm before the storm.

"You finish your juice. I'm going to the barn." Mom stands up. She hasn't touched her juice. I chug the rest of mine.

"Ready!" I hold the door open for her.

"Thanks, Petunia."

Now is not the time to complain about my dreaded nickname. "Mom, I have to tell you something . . ."

"Yes?"

I skip to keep up with her as she strides across the lawn toward the awful truth.

"Well, you know the kitten we found . . . ?"

Mom glances at me but doesn't slow down.

"And then the collar and leash?" I remember I haven't even told her about finding Hairy Pawter yet. *Probably best to leave him out of it for now.* "Well . . ." I pick up my pace to catch up. "Well . . ."

We reach the barn door, and Mom turns to me. "Yes? What is it?" When she opens the door, I can't breathe. The moment of truth.

"It's Chewy."

"What about Chewy?" Mom heads inside.

"She's gone," I blurt out. "She's at the haunted house."

Mom chuckles. "What are you talking about? She's right here."

I gape at Chewbacca. The chimp is sitting in the corner of her cage, eating a banana. How did she escape from that brick garage? She must have come back during the night. "But, where's Hairy?"

"Who?" Mom fingers the lock on Chewy's pen. "How'd she get her own banana?"

"That's what I've been trying to tell you. Chewy picked the lock on her gate."

"Clever girl." Mom laughs. I'm not sure if she means me or Chewbacca. "Get a combination lock out of the storage closet. I'm going to change this lock." Mom dumps some chimp chow in Chewy's dish. "We're going to have to start calling you Houdini." Mom is used to crazy stuff happening at the petting zoo. She takes it all in stride . . . but that's because she doesn't know the half of it.

If Chewbacca escaped, then Hairy Pawter did, too. So where is he now?

"How is she getting out?" Mom asks.

"She must have a tool . . ." I search inside her enclosure. *Aha!* A screwdriver peeks out from a pile of sawdust. Mom's right. She is a clever chimp! I stuff the screwdriver into my spy vest.

"Can you finish up here?" Mom removes her gloves and wipes her hands on her overalls. "I'm going to go check on your brother."

I nod as I attach the new combo lock to the gate.

After Mom's gone, I sit on an overturned bucket near Chewbacca's enclosure. I watch her chew her banana like nothing happened. "Where is he?" I put my elbows on my knees and my head in my hands. "Where's Hairy Pawter?" If Chewy opened the door to that garage on her own, did she close it again, leaving Hairy and the cat still locked inside? Why didn't she free them, too?

Chewbacca blinks and chews.

"You know, don't you?" Through the bars of her pen, I hand her another banana. "Why aren't you telling?" *Yikes!* I'm starting to think like Crispy, expecting the chimp to respond. Maybe I hit my head on a branch, too.

Back in my bedroom, I review my notes from the last few days.

First, Yara goes missing. Someone returns her for the reward. Then, Freddie finds a key in the wall at the bakery, along with Lyncoya's secret diary. Next, missing pets and collars and stuff start showing up in Chewbacca's pen—maybe *she's* the petnapper? Nah. She'd want to be paid in bananas, not dollars.

Mr. Swindell loses his dog, Hairy Pawter. I find Hairy in the old shack, but he goes missing again—then I find him *and* Chewy in the garage outside the haunted mansion. And now Hairy's missing again . . . unless he's still at the haunted house.

Freddie gets lost in the forest. Crispy sneaks out to search for him, not once but twice. He hits his head on a branch and ends up with stitches. Kelly Finkelman returns Freddie for the reward. *Could Kelly be the petnapper?* Maybe. She did return Freddie . . . and come to think of it, someone matching her description returned Yara, too. I make a mental note to investigate Smelly Kelly.

Last night, while looking for Hairy and Chewbacca, I find Court's tombstone in a private cemetery at the haunted mansion. It just has to be the tombstone from Lyncoya's riddle, but I still don't know what it means. At least Freddie, Chewy, and Crispy are back.

Whew. That's a lot for one pet detective! Summer vacation is off to a roaring start!

I finish up my chores in the barn—scooping the poop, throwing slop into troughs, and filling water bowls. I even do Crispy's chores, including talking to the animals. Crispy swears by Apollo's advice. But when I ask the cub what I should do, all he does is roll over on his back and purr.

When I finish up in the barn, I head back to the house. I'm starving. I hope Mom makes pancakes again.

Crispy is sitting at the kitchen table with Freddie wrapped around his neck. Mom is dishing up piping hot bowls of . . . oatmeal. *Sigh.* I smother mine in apple chunks, raisins, and cream. Anything to make it edible.

Crispy hands Freddie a chunk of apple. Balancing on Crispy's shoulders, the ferret takes the fruit in both hands and nibbles. Xavier the soccer ball has his own seat at the table.

"When is Ronny coming back?" I force myself to swallow a bite of mush. "She must be missing Xavier."

"Your father is dropping her off this morning on his way to work." Mom sits next to me and digs into her bowl of oatmeal. She eats hers plain. *Yuck.* "Kassy, I'm counting on you to watch your brother and stepsister and not get into any more trouble. I'll ask one of the vet techs to check on you throughout the day, so don't get any ideas."

I nod. I don't know why I'm responsible for keeping them out of trouble. *Just because I'm the oldest . . .*

"I have a busy day at the clinic. But I'll be right next door." I'm not sure if she's reassuring me or warning me.

"Can we go to the bakery?" I want to tell Butler what I found at the mansion. "Mrs. Patel needs our help."

"I'm sure she doesn't need you two in the way again."

"We're her gaggle." Crispy says with his mouth full. "*Kalahansa*. That means *geese* in Hindi."

Mom laughs. "You're a gaggle of geese, all right."

"So can we go to the bakery?" I scrape up the last bite and force it down. "You won't have to worry about us there. Mrs. Patel—"

"Percy are you sure you feel okay?"

"We feel great. Right, Freddie?" Crispy feeds the ferret a raisin.

Mom shakes her head. "Let me call Mrs. Patel and ask if she wants you there." She slides her phone out of her pocket.

I hold my breath, listening to Mom's side of the conversation.

"Really? You're sure it's no trouble?"

Crispy bounces up and down in his chair. He's as excited as I am.

"You're sure you want them—" Mom shifts the phone to her other ear. "All three of them? Ronny, too? Okay. Thanks." Mom shrugs. "Mrs. Patel says 'the more the merrier.' She promised to put you all to work."

"Hooray!" Crispy does a little dance, sending Freddie sliding down his back. The ferret toots in protest.

I see Dad's SUV pull into the driveway. "Ronny's here!" I jump up from the table and take my empty bowl to the sink. I hope she remembered to bring her Girl Scout cookies like I asked when I called her yesterday.

"Maybe your father can drive you to the bakery." Mom grabs her phone and taps out a text. "I don't have time." I wish she'd just walk outside and talk to him.

"Xavier!" Ronny bursts into the kitchen and heads straight for her soccer ball. She picks it up and hugs it. Xavier is to Ronny what Freddie is to Crispy. "Are you okay now, Percy?"

Crispy smiles and nods.

"You kids ready to go?" Dad peeks his head in the door. When Mom averts her eyes, I feel a stabbing in my chest.

Crispy and Ronny are playing tug-of-war over Xavier, and Freddie is squeaking. I follow them out to Dad's car. Ronny, Xavier, Crispy, and Freddie climb into the backseat, and I claim the front seat. Being the oldest has some advantages.

In the morning light, the pink-and-yellow striped awning of the bakery looks like a shiny candy wrapper. Butler and Oliver are sitting at one of the café tables, eating rice pudding and drinking chai.

"Kids!" Mrs. Patel bustles into the storefront. She has flour on her face, and her dark hair is escaping its bun. She wipes her hands on her floral apron. "Have some *kheer* and chai." She grabs a tray and places three cups on it. From a giant urn on the counter, she fills the cups with milky tea.

Crispy and Ronny sit at one café table, and I pull my chair up to the third table in the small storefront. Mrs. P delivers the tea, and we all dump a load of sugar into our cups.

Ahhh . . . The warm, sweet tea is like heaven. Mrs. P brings us each a bowl of rice pudding.

"Thanks, Mrs. P." I dig in. "Delicious as always."

"After you're done with breakfast, you kids can wipe down the tables, chairs, and display case." Mrs. P points to Crispy and Ronny. Then she turns to Butler and Oliver. "Booboo, you sweep, and Oli can help me carry the flour sacks."

"I hope Kali comes back," Butler says.

"Kali's gone?" Crispy asks.

"She didn't come home last night."

I take out my notebook and sketch a picture of Kali. Too bad I don't have a colored pencil to show her emerald green eyes. Kali is the Patel's fat black cat. *Wait a second!*

Mrs. Patel smiles. "At least someone found Mr. Swindell's dog."

I stop drawing. "When?"

"Last night."

"Who found him?" I drop my pencil. "Did they collect the reward?"

"Some girl. You'll have to ask Mr. Swindell." Mrs. Patel takes a rare break and sits down across from me. She sips a cup of chai and sighs. "The auctioneer should be here any minute."

"Auctioneer?" I ask.

"I may have to sell everything if I can't pay the rent." She slumps in her chair. "The oven quit working and the repairman is on his way. Just be glad you're not a businesswoman."

"Oh no!" I gulp a mouthful of chai.

"Don't you worry." Mrs. Patel gives me a sad sort of smile. "Everything works out for the best."

I hope she's right.

"In fact, Mr. Swindell was so happy to get his dog back that he gave me an extra week to pay." She picks up her cup and gets up from the table

Maybe this girl collecting rewards is our dog and catnapper. "I need to interview Mr. Swindell about the reward. I suspect foul play."

Mrs. P scrunches her eyebrows. "But the girl found the dog."

"The girl?"

"I remember now. Mr. Swindell mentioned it was a pretty blonde girl from your school, a cheerleader, who returned his cockapoo."

"Kelly Finkelman," I say under my breath. She's the petnapper.

17

THE PLAN

"I'VE GOT AN IDEA HOW TO GET KALI BACK." I stuff my notebook in my spy vest and stand up.

"How?" Butler asks.

"You kids can plan after your chores and lunch," Mrs. Patel says. She points to the broom.

After we help Mrs. Patel in the bakery—and eat a super yummy curry lunch—Crispy, Butler, Oliver, and Ronny meet in my office to formulate a plan to rescue Kali and find the treasure.

Crispy sits on a cardboard box, feeding Freddie cookie crumbs. Ronny marches in place in the doorway, bouncing her soccer ball on her knees. Butler sits cross-legged on the floor near the hole in the wall, probably waiting to see if anything crawls out of it. And Oliver leans against the doorframe, chewing on a straw, looking bored. The only reason he's up this early is because his mom makes him.

I lay the diary and my notebook on top of a stack of boxes. "Yesterday, I found Court's tombstone." Now I've got everyone's attention. "Well, lots of them. I'm sure this is the clue from Lyncoya's diary. We know this diary is a treasure map, and the riddles are clues. So maybe we're looking in the wrong cemetery." I unfold the map at the center of the diary. "Look." I point at an *X* in the middle of the page. "This map is two hundred years old, and Nashville has changed a lot since then. But this *X* is between a forest and a cemetery. See?"

Butler's eyes get wide. "Really?" He leans over the map.

"I think it's the cemetery I found at the haunted mansion. I'm betting that old mansion is part of what used to be Andrew Jackson's estate. That's where I saw the Court tombstones."

"Wow! You went to the haunted mansion?" Crispy jumps off the stack of boxes. "I wanna go too."

Oliver whistles through his teeth.

I pull the wooden box out of my vest pocket, open it, and hold up the antique key. "I think this key unlocks a treasure chest hidden in that cemetery."

"If we find the treasure, we can save the bakery!" Crispy claps his hands together.

"What's your plan?" Butler asks, giving his brother the stink eye.

"The third riddle is key." I pick up the diary and read out loud: "It's seen in the middle of March and April but can't be seen at the beginning or end of either month." I glance around.

"Anyone know the answer?" *Answer. Answerrr* . . . A firecrackerrr goes off in my brrrain! "The letter *R*! That's it!"

"Clever," Butler says. "In the middle of March and April."

"What an easy riddle." Oliver flips his straw at his brother. "Not clever at all.."

"It's a cool riddle," Crispy says.

"We've got to get back to that graveyard." I examine the key, then put it back in its box. Fingering the ridges on the end of the box, I think about the weird letter *R* on the Court gravestone. "There's definitely something at that tombstone."

"Let's go find the treasure." Crispy bounces up and down. Freddie holds onto his hair and squeals.

I turn to Oliver. "Can you drive us to the haunted mansion?"

"I'll go tell Mom we're going to visit our old friend Court." Oliver chuckles. He does an about-face and heads toward the kitchen.

Ronny gets a worried look on her face and hugs Xavier to her chest. "I don't want to go to some haunted mansion or creepy graveyard."

"It's not creepy," I fib. Actually, the whole place gives me the creeps . . . the house, the grounds, the weird garage, and especially the private graveyard. "Well, not that creepy. Anyway, if we get into trouble, you're a crack shot with that soccer ball."

She smiles and points to the ceiling. "Wanna see me hit the light?"

"No!" Butler and I say in unison. My office is in bad enough shape as it is. With everything going on lately, I haven't had time to straighten it up.

Butler gets up off the floor and brushes off the butt of his pants. Before he can follow Oliver, I stop him. "Wait. There's something else. I know where Kali is."

Butler gapes at me.

"She's been catnapped."

"Why would anyone steal Kali?"

"I was tracking Chewbacca and Hairy Pawter. That's how I ended up at the haunted mansion." I stuff my notebook back into my spy vest. "Anyway, on the grounds, there's an old garage, like for carriages. Chewbacca and Hairy Pawter were inside. I saw them through a window. I also saw a black cat with green eyes. It has to be Kali. But the doors were locked. So how'd they get in?"

"A portal through the space-time continuum?" Crispy kisses Freddie's nose. "Right, Freddie?"

I shake my head. "Someone put them there." I pick up the diary, wrap its leather strap around it, and slide it into the back pocket of my vest. "Our petnapper."

"But why steal pets?" Butler asks.

"For the reward. And who is collecting the rewards?"

He shrugs.

"Smelly Kelly."

"Kelly Finkelman from school?" He scrunches up his face. "The pretty cheerleader?"

"Pretty *rotten* if you ask me."

"I don't believe it. Not Kelly." Butler shakes his head. "She's one of the nicest, most popular girls at school."

"Just because you're popular doesn't mean you're nice."

"But she *is* nice," Butler says.

Yeah, right. Being gorgeous doesn't make you nice. "Maybe she has a dark side we don't know about. Like one of those celebrities who has everything but shoplifts because they're bored."

"I'm telling you, Hairy and Kali were transported into the carriage house by an alien intelligence who believes dogs and cats are the most evolved species on earth." Crispy feeds Freddie a cookie crumb. "What they haven't realized yet is *ferrets* are the superior species."

Sometimes I think my brother is an alien from another planet.

"Percy's right," Butler says.

I stare at him. Has he lost his mind? Or am I in some alternate universe?

"An alien would be more likely than Kelly Finkelman. No way she'd do something bad."

"You're blinded by her beauty," I tease. A rosy glow spreads across his brown cheeks.

Oliver reappears holding the car keys and a large box full of pastries. "Ready? Mom wants me to deliver these. But afterward, I'll swing by the haunted mansion and—"

"And catch the petnapper!" Crispy chimes in.

Ronny slips out the door.

"Where are you going?" I ask.

"To get some cookies for the road."

A tiny voice says, "Good idea."

Wait. I shake my head. *Was that Freddie?* I must be hearing things. I gawk at the ferret, who is sitting on Crispy's shoulder, washing his face with his paws. A mischievous smile stretches across my brother's freckled face.

"Okay, here are your assignments," I whisper, gesturing for everyone to gather around. *Wait? Why am I whispering?*

Ronny comes back with a handful of cookies. She passes them out.

"Ronny, you've got your soccer ball and your Girl Scout Cookies, right? And did you bring your Girl Scout sash so you look official?"

She nods and picks up her backpack. "In here."

"I've got the diary and the key." I pat the pockets of my spy vest.

"Oliver's driving the getaway car."

He jiggles the car keys.

"What about me?" Butler asks. "What's my job?"

"And me?" Crispy asks. "And Freddie?" Freddie peers over Crispy's head at me.

"You two . . . er, three, are with me." I hold my finger out and Freddie licks it. "We've got to figure out what's special about the letter *R* to find the treasure." I wipe my finger on my jeans. "Everybody ready? It could be a dangerous mission." I think of the snarling beast and the angry man who chased me yesterday. "Stay alert and be prepared."

Oliver pulls off the old highway onto a dirt road in the forest preserve. As usual, he waits with the car. The rest of us hike through the woods to the mansion.

Once I'm sure the coast is clear, I help Ronny put her Girl Scout sash over her head and send her to the front porch.

"Why can't Percy go to the door? I'm scared." Ronny digs in her heels.

"You want Percy to pretend to sell Girl Scout Cookies?"

"Why not?"

"Look, you only have to go to the door if someone comes around or asks what we're up to. You're our distraction." I point her in the direction of the house. "Otherwise, just sit on the porch and stay out of sight."

"Can Percy come with me?"

"Good idea. You and Crispy go to the front porch. If anyone comes out, try to sell them cookies and keep them distracted!"

Ronny, Xavier, Crispy, and Freddie make their way up the hill. Halfway there, Ronny and Crispy start kicking Xavier back and forth. Freddie is holding on for dear life. I shake my head. I should have known better than to bring those goofballs on this mission.

"Come on." I head through the brush for the private cemetery. Butler tags along close behind me.

The gravestones are even more dilapidated than I remembered, with stones angled every which way and some crumbled into dust.

"Here!" I swerve around a clump of weeds and squat down next to what's left of the first Court headstone, the one with the fancy letter *R*.

"Why did all these people die so young?" Butler asks. He takes out his phone and starts tapping away. "Wow!" He stares over at me with his mouth gaping open.

"What?"

"These aren't people."

My stomach does a flip-flop. *What is that supposed to mean?* I give him a questioning look.

"This isn't a people cemetery. It's a horse cemetery."

I lose my balance and fall backward onto my butt. "What?"

"Court, Lady Nashville, Bolivia . . ." Butler hands me his phone. "They were Andrew Jackson's horses."

"So Court-the-first, second, and third, are all horses?"

Butler nods.

"'Father carries a bullet next to his heart for Truxton,'" I whisper, remembering the line from Lyncoya's diary. "I wonder if Truxton is buried here."

"Who's Truxton?" Butler asks.

"Andrew Jackson's prize race horse. The one Lyncoya talks about in his diary." I explain about Truxton and the bullet.

Butler dashes from stone to stone, reading off the names of the horses.

I move closer to Court-the-first's headstone and examine the engraving. Crawling on my hands and knees, I look for anything that could be a keyhole. I just know the key Freddie found opens something in this graveyard, something Lyncoya hid here.

"Court isn't the only name with an *R* in it," Butler calls out.

"Yeah, but the first riddle led to headstone, the second to Court, and the third to R." I run my finger over the grooves in the letter R. "I think they are a kind of map, bringing us closer to the treasure." Sitting on my haunches, I take the wooden box from my pocket and remove the key. I try inserting it into the hole in the letter *R*. Nothing. Something isn't right. The top of the *R* has teethlike grooves but nothing that fits this key.

Wait a second! I run my finger around the grooves on the end of the wooden box. *Aha!*

"The box is the real key!" I angle the grooves on the end of the box to fit the teeth in the letter *R*. "It fits!" When I twist the wooden box, the front section of the tombstone gives way and opens onto a compartment inside. *Holy hideout!*

"Look at this!"

Butler rushes over to my side.

"Look at what?" A familiar voice says from behind me.

I whirl around. Slug is standing on the sidewalk, staring at me. He stomps on the end of his skateboard, it pops straight up, and he grabs it.

"Slug, what are you doing here?"

"What are *you* doing here?" He joins us at the graveside.

"I asked first."

"You found it!" Slug pushes me aside and snatches a leather pouch out of the inside of the tombstone. He whistles. "Well, lookie here." He laughs.

"I found it." I lunge at the pouch, but Slug is too fast. "Give it back!"

"Try and make me." Slug opens the leather drawstring with his teeth. *Whoa!* He lets the pouch drop to the ground and holds up an ornate gold bit shank. I recognize it because we use a bit with our pony, Morpheus. The shank is part of the bit that goes into the horse's mouth. But this one is made of gold!

"Kassy's right," Butler says. "She found it. It belongs to her."

Butler tries to grab the bit out of Slug's hand. Slug laughs and takes off running up the hill.

Butler and I take off after him.

"Ronny!" I point wildly at Slug. "Stop him!"

Ronny drops her backpack on the porch. With Xavier under her arm, she runs out onto the grass. She dropkicks the soccer ball . . . but it zips across the grass ahead of Slug.

He looks back and chuckles—right before tripping over Xavier and tumbling to the ground. *Amazing!* Ronny knew right where to kick the ball after all.

"What's going on?" Crispy runs over to Slug. Freddie jumps off my brother's shoulders and pounces on Slug. "Freddie!" Crispy dives after the ferret.

Slug rolls over, trying to swat Freddie away. "Get that rat off of me!"

"He's not a rodent!"

Freddie chirps and runs off with a single key that must have fallen out of Slug's pocket.

Still running full tilt, I slide to a stop when I trip over Slug's legs. *There it is!* The golden bit. It's lying in the grass. I scramble on hands and knees and grab it.

Slug kicks at me with his feet.

"Jamie!" A woman's voice calls from porch. "Quit roughhousing and invite your friends in for some lemonade."

18
ROCK STARS

WE ALL STARE DOWN AT SLUG. He just lies there on the grass, gaping up at the sky.

"Jamie?" I raise my eyebrows. *Maybe he's not such a tough guy after all.*

The thin woman calls again: "Jamie, I want to meet your friends." She's standing on the porch shielding her eyes from the sun with her hand.

Slug sits up.

"Is that your foster mom?" Butler asks.

Slug doesn't answer. He jumps up and brushes off his pants. Hoping he doesn't notice, I slip the golden bit into my vest pocket.

"Jamie!" the woman calls again. "Come on in now, son. And bring your friends. I made chocolate chip cookies."

Slug's cheeks are red. He waves at her. "Want to come in?" he mumbles. The words sound like marbles rolling around in his mouth.

"Sure." Ronny scoops up her soccer ball. "Chocolate chip is my favorite!"

"Okay. Why not?" I don't want cookies, but I do want information. I have my reasons for being curious about Slug... *Why would he look exactly like a younger version of his foster mom?*

The woman disappears back into the house.

"Come on, then." Slug sighs. Like a boy called to the principal's office, he hangs his head as he walks toward the house.

"Wait!" I glance around. "Where's Crispy?"

He must have taken off after Freddie. Now they're nowhere to be seen. *Not again!*

"Percy!" I call out as I race down the hill in the direction Freddie ran with Slug's key in the direction of the carriage garage. My brother just got out of the hospital. I'm supposed to be taking care of him. I already lost him once this week. I'd better not lose him again. It's Freddie's fault. Crispy should keep that ferret on a leash.

Frantic, I trip over my own feet and do a face-plant on the lawn.

"Are you okay?" As usual, Butler's right behind me. He offers me a helping hand. I take it and spit out a mouthful of grass. *Tastes like Mom's zucchini cake.*

Ronny giggles. "Your shirt has a big green streak."

Not another shirt ruined. Mom's going to have a cow. "Look!" I point to the carriage house.

With Slug's key still in his mouth, Freddie is pawing at the door. Down on all fours at ferret-level, Crispy is trying to reason with him. They look like two dogs begging to get in.

Freddie chirps and digs at the door. Whatever's inside, that crazy ferret really wants it.

Hurrying over, I stare down at Crispy and Freddie, my two little brothers, in trouble as usual. Freddie looks up at me with his beady black eyes and drops the key. I pick it up. It's all wet and slimy with ferret spit. I wipe it off on my pants.

I insert the key in the doorknob lock and open the door. The place is creepy with cobwebs, and old fashioned horse carriages with peeling paint. Everything inside looks old. It even smells old, like hundred-year-old dust.

Freddie runs inside, and Crispy follows him.

At the far end of the cluttered room, I spot a box of dog biscuits and a giant bag of dog food.

Freddie makes a beeline for the box of biscuits and helps himself.

"Dog biscuits!" Crispy and I say in unison. Freddie loves dog biscuits.

I scan the garage. Is the cat still here? "Kitty, kitty." I squat down to look under one of the old carriages.

"Kali!" Butler snaps his fingers. The cat appears out from the wheel hub of the carriage. Kali rubs against Butler's legs and meows. He bends down and scoops her into his arms. "Kali—we found you!" The cat licks his face . . . another sloppy reunion. Ronny joins in petting the cat.

Freddie helps himself to the dog biscuits. Crispy joins him on the floor, thankfully not eating biscuits—although my brother's been known to eat dog biscuits before he became a vegetarian.

Slug appears in the doorway. "What are you guys doing in here?"

"You're the one who has some answering to do." I take out my notebook and pencil. "Why is Mrs. Patel's cat locked in your garage?"

"I have no idea."

"What about Chewbacca and Hairy Pawter? I saw them in here yesterday."

Slug shrugs. "No clue."

Then it dawns on me. When we saw Slug in the woods, he knew Freddie had been found before I did. *How could he have known that? Unless . . .*

"When we saw you in the woods with Spittoon, how'd you know Freddie had been found?"

Slug tightens his lips.

"You couldn't have known, unless *you* found him."

Slug just blinks.

"You took him for the reward money, didn't you?"

"Why would I keep the measly twenty-five dollar reward your mom offered?"

"How'd you know the reward was twenty-five dollars?"

His mouth drops open, but he doesn't say anything. Then he shakes his head. "Anyway, it wasn't me. Kelly Finkelman collected the reward."

"And how do you know that?"

"Hey Jamie!" A perky voice interrupts my interrogation.

Speak of the deviled egg. It's Smelly Kelly in the pretty pink flesh. Her shiny blond hair is pulled into a ponytail, and she's wearing a cute purple skirt. Everything about her is cute.

I give her the stink eye. "So you two are friends?"

"Jamie's taking me out for ice cream." When Kelly twirls around, her skirt pinwheels.

"What? But he's fourteen and you're—"

"Special," she says with a smirk. Kelly Finkelman is twelve going on twenty.

A firecracker goes off in my brain: *They're working together. Slug steals the pets, and Kelly returns them for the rewards. Devious!*

"Jamie!" the woman's voice sounds closer.

She appears in the doorway. With wavy brown hair flopping in her face and deep blue eyes, she's a lady version of Slug—like a member of one of those boy bands Smelly Kelly goes gaga over. "Are you kids ready for some lemonade and cookies?"

As she glances around the garage, her smile disappears. "What's going on in here? Why all the dog food?"

"Jamie is rescuing strays," Kelly says in a singsong voice.

Stealing them, more like!

"Not again." She gives Slug the side-eye. "We'll talk about this later. Right now, why don't you all come up to the house?"

"Yes, please!" Ronny has Xavier in one hand. She's still petting Kali with the other.

"Thanks, Mrs. Harrison." Kelly smiles her sweetest just-for-parents smile. "Jamie's parents are famous musicians," she says proudly.

"You're not a foster kid?" Crispy asks, as we're walking up to the house.

Mrs. Harrison laughs. "Not that old story again, Jamie." She shakes her head. "You're incorrigible."

Luckily, I'm past the letter *I* in the dictionary. *Incorrigible* means persistent or hopeless.

So, Slug—a.k.a. Jamie Harrison, son of famous musicians—has been pulling the wool over our eyes with his story about being an orphan. *But why? Why would he make up stories? And if his parents live in that mansion, why would he need the reward money?*

The mansion isn't dark and spooky like I expected. Inside, it's light and sleek and smells like fresh-baked cookies. *Wow! Why did I think this was a haunted house?* They must have remodeled it. *When did they even move in?*

I feel like I'm walking through a home-decorating magazine. Black-and-white photographs of musicians hang on the walls, and all the furniture is white. Mrs. Harrison leads us through a huge foyer, past the living room, into a shiny stainless steel kitchen. On the table, bloodred roses sit in a white vase. It's the only shock of color in the house.

I pull up a heavy upholstered chair, trying not to smudge the smooth glass table. I glare at Crispy when he puts his grubby hands on the table. Freddie stands on my brother's shoulders, gazing around the room, probably looking for something to eat. Ronny puts Xavier down on a chair and sits next to him. It. *Whatever.*

Slug slumps into a chair across the table from me, which is handy since I plan to interrogate him. Kelly sits next to him and flashes her perfect smile. *Good.* I have a few questions for her, too.

The muscles pop out on Mrs. Harrison's arms as she carries a big silver tray to the table. She's really fit. She must work out a lot or play a lot of tennis. She pours lemonade out of a crystal pitcher and sets a glass in front of each of us, then passes around a plate of cookies. *Yum!*

A giant black dog follows her, wagging its tail.

"What kind of dog is that? It looks like a bear." That must be the beast I saw the other day.

"She's a Newfoundland. And her name is Bear." Mrs. Harrison laughs. "She's sweet when you get to know her."

"She likes people, but she hates other dogs," Slug adds.

Bear sniffs at Freddie. I hope she doesn't decide the ferret looks like a yummy snack.

The first bite of warm cookie almost makes me forget why I'm here.

"Lucky coincidence you found both Hairy Pawter and Freddie and collected both rewards," I say to Kelly.

"Jamie found them." The way she grins at Slug, all moon-eyed, makes me want to barf.

"Found them or took them?"

Slug sits up in his chair. "What? You think I stole them?" He narrows his eyes.

"Did you?"

He laughs. "Do you always assume the worst?"

"Conclusions, not assumptions. A good detective sets aside her assumptions and uses logic to reach conclusions." I wave my cookie at him. "Do you always answer a question with another question?"

"Only when the questions are bonkers."

I take another bite of cookie and glare at him.

"What's this about stealing?" Mrs. Harrison asks as she pulls a chair up to the table. "Jamie?"

The way she says his name suggests this isn't the first time he's been in trouble.

"Some neighbors' pets went missing and I found them. That's all."

Mrs. Harrison's phone sings some funky song. She slips it out of the back pocket of her jeans. "Sorry. It's my agent," she says as she gets up from the table and disappears into the other room.

"Kassy's the pet detective," Crispy chimes in.

"Exactly." Slug smirks. "And how many lost pets did she find?"

I gulp a mouthful of lemonade. "I found Hairy Pawter."

"You mean your monkey found Hairy Pawter." Slug points a cookie at me. "But only after I'd already found him."

"And instead of returning Hairy Pawter or Chewbacca, you locked them up in the garage. Were you waiting for a reward?"

"Like I need a reward for a monkey." Slug scoffs.

"Chewy's not a monkey." Crispy puts his glass down a little too hard, and it makes a loud bang. "She's a chimp. Monkeys have tails. Hominids don't."

"Well, your chimp is a better pet detective than your sister."

"We're a team," Crispy says. "Chewy, Freddie, Spittoon, Ronny, Butler, me . . ." He breaks off a piece of cookie and hands it to Freddie.

"Crispy's right." I nod. "And unlike you, we were going to give the rewards to Mrs. Patel." I finger the gold shank bit in my pocket and wonder if it's worth enough to save the bakery.

"Unlike me?" Slug shakes his head. "There you go making assumptions again."

"Jamie's a pet detective, too," Kelly says. "A good one."

"Since when are you a pet detective?" I narrow my eyes at him. "Pet *thief*, more like."

"I just came from Patel Pastries." Kelly pulls a pink-and-yellow napkin from her princess purse. "Jamie asked me to deliver the reward money, all $225." She opens the napkin and holds out a golden shortbread cookie. "Mrs. Patel gave me this." She offers it to Slug. "I was saving it to share with you."

"What?" My head is spinning. "You gave the reward money to Mrs. Patel?"

Slug leans back in his chair and grins at me. "When I first met you at the bakery, you said you were going to collect rewards to save the bakery. But you made it clear you didn't want my help." He's leaning back so far that his chair balances on two legs. "So I decided to collect the rewards myself." *Bang!* He lets his chair fall to the floor. "And show you who is the greatest pet detective."

"But you lied about being an orphan. And you tried to take the diary. And you—"

"People go nuts when they find out my parents are rock stars." Slug blushes. "*The Harrisons.*" He makes air quotes with his fingers. "I just want to fit in like a normal kid . . . to be part of the team." He pushes a cookie off the plate onto the table. "You promised to meet me at the bakery and let me help with the diary, but you didn't show up."

I'm not going to let Slug change the subject. "So you found the pets? You didn't steal them?"

He nods.

"But why didn't you give them back right away? And why did you lock them in that stinky old garage?"

170

"I told you, Bear doesn't like other dogs . . . or any other animals. Except humans."

"She likes Freddie," Crispy says with his mouth full of cookie. "Everyone likes Freddie."

"Everyone except Stinkerton Killjoy." I sip my lemonade. "Good thing we found him and the other animals before Stinkerton did. We should be glad of that anyway."

"What about Yara?" Ronny turns to Slug. "Did you find her, too?"

"Who's Yara?"

"My shih tzu puppy."

Slug shakes his head.

"She smells like strawberries and wears a bow." I take out my notebook and flip to a page with a sketch of Yara. "And when it rains, she wears little black rubber boots. She's about the size of a soccer ball and like a soccer ball, she's black and white."

Slug looks at the picture. "Nope, I didn't find her."

"Maybe there's another pet detective!" Crispy says.

"Or another petnapper!" Ronny grabs another cookie off the plate.

It's true. There could be another petnapper. Slug might not be the only one "finding" animals for reward money. Anyway, Yara was taken in downtown Nashville, a ten-minute drive from here. And Slug doesn't have a car. So unless he stole the animals and brought them home on the bus or in an Uber . . . there must be another dognapper still at large.

"Jamie, why don't you take your friends down to the playroom?" Mrs. Harrison starts clearing the dishes from the table. "You can show them your karaoke machine."

"You guys want to do karaoke?" Slug's cheeks turn pink again. "Or we could play Ping-Pong."

"You have a Ping-Pong table?" Crispy's eyes get wide.

Slug nods. "And a pool table."

Crispy looks at me. "Kassy?"

Butler's phone buzzes. He glances at it. "Dang." He gives a little laugh. "I forgot—Oliver's waiting at the car."

"You might as well invite him in to play pool," Slug says.

Butler smiles. "If you play pool with Oliver, you might regret it."

19

OFF TO WASHINGTON!

THE NEXT SUNDAY, SLUG'S PARENTS—the famous rock stars—hold a benefit concert for Mrs. Patel's bakery. It's a sunny summer afternoon, and everyone in Lemontree Heights shows up to help out. Watching the crowd from a distance reminds me of Crispy's worm farm. What you see depends on your perspective, I guess.

Mrs. Patel is beaming as she passes out Indian treats from a pink-and-yellow striped tent set up on the lawn. Wearing thin blue plastic gloves, Butler, Oliver, and Slug offer cookies and barfi to folks milling around listening to the music.

I grab a square of barfi off a silver tray and notice the rubber toe of a red sneaker peeking out from under the

table. When I take a bite of the sweet dessert, it crumbles. Half falls to the ground. Like a jack-in-the-box, a ferret paw pops out from under the table and snatches it. I should have known Crispy and Freddie would be near the food.

"Hey, Kassy," Slug smirks. "Found any lost pets lately?"

I tip my fedora. "I'm a pet detective. That's what I do."

"Did you hear the Nashville police caught a guy who was stealing dogs from pet groomers?" Slug asks.

"What?" So there *is* another dognapper. *I knew it!*

Slug just laughs.

I'm still not sure about the guy. He tried to grab the diary and the golden bit bag away from me. *I mean, they didn't really belong to* me, *either* . . . Still, that's no reason to be so grabby. And did he really *find* all those pets or did he take them? I guess giving the reward money to Mrs. Patel is a point in his favor. But it was still wrong.

I hear Crispy's voice in my head: *Apollo says we shouldn't profit from the misery of others.* For a cougar cub, I guess he's pretty smart. I grab a couple shortbread cookies for the road and make my way out of the crowd.

I guess I feel kind of sorry for Slug. This morning, I overheard Mrs. Harrison talking to Mom about "sending him back to therapy." I hope it works. He's really not so bad once you get to know him.

I wander around the edge of the Harrison's property until I find myself at the private cemetery. It's surrounded by yellow tape and DO NOT ENTER signs. A team from the archeology department at Vanderbilt University has taken over the site.

Archeologists study old buried treasures and use them to figure out how people lived in the past.

I wanted to sell the gold bit to help Mrs. Patel pay her rent. But Mom made me give it to the Harrisons since I found it on their property and it belongs to them. Mrs. Harrison donated it to the Andrew Jackson Museum. She says it's a "piece of history" and belongs to everyone.

Munching on a cookie, I stare into the graveyard. I wonder what they'll learn about Lyncoya from the treasures inside the tombstone. Maybe there are more tricky headstones filled with treasures. Mom made me hand over the diary, the key, and the trick box. *Sigh.* It's kind of sad. Lyncoya was like a friend and my constant companion for the last week. I miss him.

A soccer ball bounces off my foot, bringing me back from my daydream.

Dad teases me about daydreaming. He says I'm a dreamer, not a doer. But how do you know what you want to do without dreaming first? Anyway, I'd say I've done a lot in the last few weeks.

"What are you doing?" Ronny asks.

"Thinking." I pick up the ball and hand it to her.

"Why?"

I shield my eyes from the bright sunshine and squint at her. "Don't you ever just think about things?"

She shakes her head and bounces Xavier on her knee.

"That explains a lot," I laugh.

"Aren't you excited Daddy is taking us camping?" Ronny spins around and catches her soccer ball before it hits the ground. "We're going to Shenandoah National Park. That's in Virginia."

I cringe. I'm still not used to her calling *my* father "daddy."

"Yeah," I say, staring down at my sandals. I think of the summer trips we used to make as a family—Mom, Dad, Crispy, Freddie, and me. Next week will be my first summer trip without Mom. It's going to be weird.

"We're going geocaching!" Ronny dribbles the ball with her feet.

Sounds like a slot machine. "What's geo-cha-ching?" I must have passed it in the dictionary by now, but I don't remember it. I need to pay more attention to my vocabulary.

"Geocaching." She rests a foot on Xavier and slips her cell phone out of the pocket of her shorts. "I'll show you." She taps the phone a few times. "See!"

I shake my head. *Again, I ask: is it fair that Ronny has her own phone and I don't?*

She points the phone at me.

"All I see is a map with lots of dots on it." I take the phone and look closer. "Is this where we are now?"

Ronny nods. "There's a cache nearby."

"A cache?" *Aha! Not cash,* cache. They're homonyms—they sound the same but have different meanings.

"Like a hidden treasure." Ronny grabs her phone back. "This app tells you coordinates where stuff is hidden."

"Who hides it?"

"People."

"What people?"

"Whoever wants to play." Walking around the cemetery, Ronny stares down at her phone like an adventurer with a compass.

"It's a game?" I follow her, peeking over her shoulder at the screen.

She ducks under the tape surrounding the cemetery.

"Wait!" I glance around to make sure no one is watching. "We're not supposed—"

"Over here!" She points to a tilted headstone in the corner of the graveyard, closest to the road. She gently taps Xavier with her foot. The soccer ball glides alongside her like a dog on a leash.

She stops and stares down at a crumbling headstone.

I stand next to her. "Where is it?"

Hands on knees, she bends over and surveys the ground.

I squat down and scan the area around the headstone. "What are we looking for?"

"Something out of place."

Holy hideaway! "I see it!" A purple plastic Easter egg is nestled up against the tombstone.

I reach out, but Ronny snatches it up first. I need to work on my reflexes too. She raises the plastic egg above her head, about to smash it on the headstone.

"No!" I shout. You'll break it."

"I'm opening it."

"*Crushing* it, more like."

Sometimes Ronny is like a bulldozer. I grab the egg out of her hands and examine it. It's a little dirty but looks pretty new. When I twist the plastic halves open, a square of paper falls out, along with a tiny silver koala bear charm.

Ronny grabs the koala, and I pick up the paper.

"Kiki the koala started her journey in Canberra, Australia," I read from the paper. "She has always wanted to visit her relatives in the Smithsonian National Zoo. Help her get to Washington!" I glance over at Ronny. "How'd Kiki get here from Australia?"

"Kiki's a travel bug!"

I blink.

"A hitchhiker!"

I blink again.

"Come on." Ronny grabs my hand. "We have to help her get to Washington!"

Crispy appears out of nowhere. "What's that?" He points at the purple egg.

"Kiki's geocache." I hurry to keep up with Ronny. Now we're all jogging.

"Who's Kiki?"

I hold up the koala charm. "This bear wants to get to the National Zoo in Washington DC."

"Hey, maybe Dad will take us there next week." Crispy stuffs Freddie into his shirt.

"But we're camping in Shenandoah National Park." Ronny drop-kicks Xavier. "Not Washington."

"Shenandoah National Park is in Virginia, and that's next to Washington. We can go camping *and* take Kiki to DC." Freddie peeks his nose out of Crispy's shirt and squeaks in agreement. "I've read that they have black-footed ferrets at the Smithsonian." Crispy kisses Freddie's nose.

"Don't worry, little bear," I say, cradling the koala charm in my palm. "We'll get you to Washington."

Ronny takes off running after Xavier. "Hooray!" she shouts. "We're going to Washington!"

I run after her. Crispy skips alongside me, with Freddie bouncing up and down in his shirt. I lock arms with Ronny and Crispy, and now we're all skipping and shouting.

"We're going to Washington!"

I can't wait. Kassy O'Roarke, pet detective, treasure hunter, and geocaching adventurer is going to Washington.

ACKNOWLEDGEMENTS

THANKS TO LISA WALSH for gently editing the roughest draft. Thanks to Barb Goffman for her first-rate edit on the second draft. And thanks to the team at Beaver's Pond—Hanna, Paige, and Athena—for cleaning up the final draft and whipping it into shape. Thanks to the three Mouseketeers—Mischief, Mayhem, and Flan—whose pawful rewrites are appreciated even if they have to be deleted. As always, thanks to Beni, my partner in quarantine and everything else.

ABOUT THE AUTHOR

KELLY OLIVER is award-winning, bestselling author of three mysteries series: *The Jessica James Mysteries*, the middle grade *Kassy O'Roarke, Pet Detective Mysteries*, and historical cozies *The Fiona Fig Mysteries*. She is Distinguished Professor of Philosophy at Vanderbilt University. To learn more about Kelly and her books, visit her website with your parent or guardian at www.kellyoliverbooks.com.

If you liked *Kassy O'Roarke, Cub Reporter* ask your parents to leave a review of the book. Reviews help Kassy and her friends keep going on adventures!

THE LAST LANDING

Richard Smith
Kristie Hold

THE LAST LANDING

ONE

Fred Noonan was not a frail or weak man, but now his body seemed to be going through a major crisis. The navigator's face appeared chalky white and droplets of perspiration crisscrossed his brow. His upper torso jerked with a gripping spasm as he turned, his eyes wide, silently pleading for help; then he let out a low-pitched moan and slumped forward in the right seat.

"Fred, what's wrong – what's going on? Oh, God, this can't be happening!"

The panicked pilot brought the twin engine plane down low over the ocean and banked toward the beach. Her frantic voice echoed through the thick air in the cockpit. "We're going in, Fred – please, I need you to stay with me!"

Both Pratt & Whitney radial engines had been feathered minutes earlier. With all the tanks dry, there was no fuel left to keep them running. The Electra had become a very heavy glider. The sound of the morning air streaming across the aluminum fuselage was the only audible indication of forward movement.

The gear came down on the descending plane as it swept over the green surf. At fifteen feet above the beach, the nose of the Electra flared and went up as the tail came down. The plane banked right and dropped hard. The wheels suspended under the wings plowed into the wet sand with a vengeance. The aircraft bounced once, and then hit the sand again, this time shearing off the right landing gear. The fuselage spun to starboard, the left wing cutting through a grove of short palm trees. Then all movement stopped and there was total silence.

The pilot stared through the broken windscreen for a few seconds, trying to collect her thoughts. Her head ached and she could feel the warm blood running down her face. On the edge of consciousness, she slowly looked over at her friend and navigator, his body still slumped in the right seat.

With her vision blurring and quickly fading to black, Amelia Earhart knew that Fred Noonan was dead.

TWO

Amelia felt a strange sensation on her cheek and the smell of decayed flesh. She imagined that something sinister was licking the blood from her face – she seemed to be having a dream – a dream that some wild animal was in the cockpit with her. She had to blink several times and squint her eyes before the wrinkled face of a nightmare finally came into focus. Amelia's eyes went wide and she immediately pushed her body back in the seat as far as she could. Her heart raced and her stomach came into her throat. She was staring into the black eyes of a huge lizard whose leathery head bobbed up and down just inches from her cheek. The creature's forked tongue reached out for her face again. She wanted to scream, but only a thin wisp of air left her lungs; her voice was being suppressed by sheer terror. A *Komodo Dragon*, she thought, as the creature opened its mouth. She could see that the teeth were serrated and angled back for ripping and tearing away flesh.

The terrified pilot instinctively reached to her waist for her survival knife. Pulling the knife up in a quick, sweeping motion, Amelia connected with the dragon's neck. The cut was superficial and not deep, but the creature's head went up and its body fell back. Thick droplets of black blood sprayed across Amelia's right hand. The wounded lizard rolled off the nose of the aircraft and dropped back into the thick brush.

Leaning forward against her shoulder harness, with the knife still raised, Amelia's hand began to shake as she realized what had just taken place. Adrenalin and fear raced through her body, but she was determined not to panic. She had never allowed the difficulties in her life to be insurmountable, and she would press forward through this one. Things were coming back to her now. Amelia remembered flying on a 'sun line' drawn by Fred, at an altitude of 1,000 feet, and she remembered the large low clouds that cast long shadows across the blue water – every shadow the shape of a small island. She remembered sending a final radio message to Howland Island on 6210 kilocycles just before the plane's tanks ran dry. Howland Island was to be her intermediate fueling stop before she arrived in Hawaii. She never received an answer from any of her desperate radio messages to the island. She had also tried to contact the "Itasca", a U.S. Coast Guard vessel stationed off the island to direct and guide her in. During the last two desperate hours her radio had become an instrument for broadcasting only. She never received even a faint reply from the island or the Coast Guard ship and she finally ran out of time and fuel. Amelia was about to put the plane down in the water when the thin slip of land appeared through the low clouds. The island below her had none of the physical characteristics of Howland and she knew that she had missed her designated landing spot. Even though she was now finally down, and thanked God for that miracle, she still had no idea where she was. All Amelia knew was that she and Fred had crashed landed on a remote beach somewhere in the Pacific – and Fred was dead.

A growing pain began to ripple through her body, and she started to realize how badly she'd been injured. Her head was bleeding less, but her chest ached and her throbbing right foot seemed to be pinned against the bottom of the instrument panel. Even though she knew that all the fuel tanks were empty, the distinct smell of aviation fuel lingered throughout the cockpit. She knew that she had to get out of the aircraft and somehow also bring Fred's body out.

Tying her flying scarf around her head, Amelia used both hands to pull her right leg free. The pain was intense and part of her flying boot tore away as she felt her right foot suddenly dislodge from the twisted metal beneath the instrument panel. She released the latch on the overhead escape hatch and pushed the two foot square door upward. The warm rays of the afternoon sun pored down across her face and seemed to give her renewed strength while reaffirming that she was actually alive. Standing on her seat, and balancing on her uninjured left foot, Amelia managed to pull her body through the hatch and slide down the side of the fuselage to the broken left wing. Fred would have to stay in the cockpit until she could open the main door at the rear of the fuselage. After re-entering the aircraft from the aft door, she would have to crawl forward across the top of the empty fuel tanks to the cockpit. If she was able, she would then pull Fred's limp body back across the tops of the tanks before finally dragging him through the rear door.

As she stood on the wing and leaned back against the wrinkled side of the Electra, she watched the blood from her right foot seep through what was left of her flying boot. She stared at the small pool of blood as it formed on the wing's surface, quickly running down the trailing edge and dripping into the sand. *I'm going to bleed out through my boot*! she thought in a panic; but the blood from the cut had already started to congeal in the hot sun. She watched as the steady bleeding finally slowed to a trickle.

She sat on the edge of the wing and removed what was left of her boot. She used her knife to cut the left sleeve from her blouse and folded the thin material together to form a bandage for her foot. She knew that once back inside the plane, she would have access to medical supplies, food and even spare clothing, but just the thought of removing Fred's body from the aircraft was overwhelming.

Leaving the safety of the wing, she limped across the sand to the rear door of the Electra and pressed down on the release lever. The door slung outward but only for a few inches. It seemed to have been jammed by the crash. Amelia pulled as hard as she could on the damaged door but only managed to open up a narrow 18" space. She squeezed through the crack and moved slowly in the dark to the supply cabinet by Fred's chart table. As she opened the cabinet's tall door, every dislodged item inside fell across her feet. She screamed out as a heavy object landed on her injured right foot. She knew that she had just encountered one of the two heavy flashlights previously stored in the cabinet. Now with the light, she was able to see and access everything scattered about the rear deck of the fuselage. Her light caught the glistening floor and she realized that two of the three, 5 gallon fresh water containers had ruptured. Most of the food rations seemed dry and intact and the first aid cabinet had survived. A small foot locker containing clothing and survival gear also seemed to be okay. Amelia opened the first aid cabinet and removed the items she would need for her injured head and foot. Next, she secured new boots from the locker along with a fresh change of clothing and a military back pack. She realized that the airplane would have to be her base of operations for a while and she was felling good about that.

Amelia wrapped her right foot in two layers of gauzed bandages and put on a light weight jacket from the supply locker. Even in the stagnant heat of the plane's interior, she felt a series of chills wash over her body. She was shaking from fear and shock, but she knew that she had to keep going. It was absolutely the last thing she wanted to do, but Amelia realized that she could no longer wait to remove Fred's body from the cockpit.

Crawling across the top of the big interior fuel tanks, she shone the broad beam from the flashlight forward toward the nose of the plane. She saw the fractured wind screen first, then the hanging overhead console. Wires and cables dangled in the light like petrified snakes. She pulled herself forward slowly across the plywood catwalk that had been laid across the tops of the rectangular tanks. Her entire body ached and her right foot throbbed but she was almost there. The yellow beam from her flashlight finally filled the cockpit – Amelia sucked in a deep breath and held it. Fred Noonan's body was gone.

THREE

Amelia could see that Fred had been pulled from the cockpit through the left side of the fractured windscreen. Scraps of his kaki coveralls hung to the broken glass and swayed like sea moss in a magnolia tree. His harness had been chewed through and shredded in several places. His seat had been pushed back and dislodged from its floor rails. Gasping and putting her right hand over her mouth, Amelia knew immediately what had happened to her copilot and navigator. The lizard had come back.

A trail of blood was painted on the curved nose of the Electra and led straight into the dense palm grove. Amelia could not believe what she was looking at. A creature from the jungle had snatched up Fred's body and slithered away with it. Now, her mind began to question every decision she had ever made about taking this dangerous journey. *This was not how it was supposed to end.* "I'm so sorry, Fred," she said as a sad mist formed in her tired eyes.

Amelia quickly wiped the tears away with the back of her hand and took in a deep breath. *If I'm not strong*, she thought, *I'll surely die here*. She knew that there were no firearms on board the plane because she would not allow it – she felt that pistols and rifles were just too big a risk and liability to be carried across five continents and fourteen countries. Fred had argued with Amelia about carrying his favorite pistol, an old military Colt '45'; "It was my father's during WWI," he had pleaded, but Amelia had simply smiled her famous smile and shook her head. Now she wished that she had allowed Fred to bring the old Colt on board. She did remember that the plane carried a flare pistol, and decided to make the signal gun a part of her backpack inventory. She knew that she would need to venture out as soon as she was physically able.

Four days after Fred disappeared; she was still nursing her right foot. The swelling had gone down substantially and she was able to squeeze into the new boot without total discomfort. She decided to leave the plane the next morning and explore the jungle nearest the beach. She had no intention of straying too far inland, but finding fresh water was now a primary objective. Even with rationing the water she had, she knew it would not last more than a month.

Gathering up what provisions she thought she'd need for the brief exploration, Amelia packed the backpack with food, and medical supplies. She threw the flare gun in on top of everything else. Her survival belt held her knife and small canteen. At the last minute, she had lashed a long machete to her canvas belt. The more she thought about the big lizard, the more she realized the creature could not have possibly been a Komodo Dragon. The island where the rare dragons lived was in Indonesia, a thousand miles away, just north of Australia. She remembered flying over the small island of Komodo on her way to New Guinea, but that was more than two days earlier. She realized that the giant lizard that took Fred was certainly not a Komodo, and she shuttered to think what the creature might have actually been.

At 7:00 a.m., on the fifth day, Amelia left the sanctuary of the downed aircraft and headed slowly inland. She moved with caution and apprehension across the thick sand and through the thickening scrub brush. Her right foot still ached and she limped along with the help of a cane that she had fashioned from the broken limb of a Quilt Grass tree.

Finding fresh water was her main goal, but finding human life would even be better. She knew that she and Fred had evidently crashed landed on a small uncharted island somewhere near her designated landing field on Howland Island, but that's all she knew. She had tried to utilize the radio in the crashed plane, but the batteries for the wireless were dead and now totally corroded by the salt air. There was a small generator on board the plane but it was destroyed in the crash. With no means to communicate with the outside world, Amelia knew that her best chance of survival was to find the island's inhabitants, or at least flag down a passing ship or aircraft.

"They're looking for me," she talked out loud as she labored through the thick underbrush, "I know that they are looking for me. After I find water, I'll go back to the beach and set up a system of

SOS signals." She smiled as she nodded her approval of the idea. She'd spell out the three-letter distress code across the beach and set up fire pits for day and night signaling. "By now, they're all looking for me," she said again, "they'll find me soon." Her right foot continued to throb within her new boot. "I know in my heart that they will find me soon."

Amelia stopped for a moment and leaned forward on her cane. She knew that her foot was beginning to swell and that she could not continue forward much longer. She was terrified of infection and the possibility of gangrene. Amelia looked through the jungle canopy at the morning sky and shielded her eyes from the rising sun.

"Please, dear God, let them find me soon."

FOUR

Turning to make her way back to her plane, Amelia spotted movement through the low brush ahead. Focusing on the moving brown object that had stopped beneath a tall palm tree, she could see that it was a small animal, maybe a deer. She moved closer for a better look. The animal had its head down as if feeding off the grass on the jungle floor. Then she saw that the animal was actually drinking water from a small stream. Her heart raced with excitement. She had been ready to turn around and now she had the source of water she needed. Plus, she also knew that small game must occupy the island along with the monster lizards. She clapped her hands and the small animal scurried off into the brush.

Amelia limped toward the stream and marveled at how clear the water was. She cupped her hands and brought the cool water to her mouth. Gulping the water from her shaking hands, she felt a sensation wash through her body that she had never felt before – similar to that first sip of wine that warms the heart, but this feeling was much more intense. She felt rejuvenated and removed her canteen from her belt. She poured out the stale water from the aluminum container and placed the empty vessel in the flowing water. It was then she saw the reflection – the reflection of the same monster she had fought off in the cockpit of the Electra. The lizard raised its head and hissed. Amelia could see the shallow scar running across its leathery neck.

Slowly backing away from the stream, Amelia reached for the machete hanging low on her belt. The lizard watched Amelia intently with its dark eyes, finally moving slowly forward. It lowered its enormous head down level with its shouldered blades, a sign that it was ready to launch an attack.

Just as Amelia raised the machete's blade, the lizard lunged across the narrow creek. The creature's eight foot long body splashed forward through the water as Amelia tumbled backward against the creek bank. She brought the blade down as hard as she could but she misjudged the forward movement of the attacking reptile. The creature was just inches away from her face when its head collapsed at her feet and its body went limp. The shaft of a long arrow protruded from its chest; the arrow's shining metal tip exposed on the other side of the dead animal's body.

Amelia lay on her back looking at the dead animal, her body raised slightly, supported by her elbows. She held the machete out in front of her, ready to defend herself against the wild native that surely would be coming for her next.

"You don't have to thank me, Miss, but I was hoping that you wasn't going to kill me."

The man with the bow stood between two palm trees and held a toothy smile. He was dressed in tattered shorts, sandals, a leather hat, and an open sleeveless shirt. A necklace of white animal teeth graced his tanned neck.

Amelia stared speechless at the apparition standing in front of her. The tall man was certainly no island native and he spoke English with a distinct Australian accent. "Who are you, and how did you get here?" she finally managed to say.

Holding the smile, the man moved closer, throwing the bow across his shoulder. He squatted beside her and put his index finger on the tip of the machete. He gently pressed downward until the blade disappeared into the grass. "Seems like a very appropriate question," he answered, "and one I could also ask of you, Miss; We don't get too many 'Shelas' around here."

"You sound Australian," Amelia said, still on the defensive.

"Born in New South Wales on the border with Queensland, Miss." he answered, removing his hat; "You've got a keen ear for dialect." He reached his hand out. "Let me help you back to your feet."

Amelia accepted the calloused hand and wondered what she was getting herself into. "Are we near Howland Island?" she asked as she stood. She noticed that the pain in her foot was almost gone.

The man with the bow scratched his short beard and blinked a few times. "I know that Island, Miss, down below the Marshals, but we ain't nowhere near it. Could it be that you've lost your way?"

Amelia thought about the remark and contemplated this strange man that had saved her life.

She was more lost than he would ever know. "I was flying to Howland when my plane went down," she said, now able to put her weight fully on her injured foot. "I was hoping that…"

The stranger put his hand in the air and closed his eyes for a second as he interrupted her. "Hold tight right there, Miss, you said that you were flying – flying what?"

Of course, he probably didn't know, she thought. "A twin engine aircraft made by Lockheed," she replied. "We were on the last leg of a trip around the world – flying from New Guinea to Honolulu, with a fuel stop at Howland Island. Somehow we ended up here."

"Good story, Miss," the man said as he retuned his hat to his head and removed a knife from his belt. "That's a damn good story," he added as he approached the dead lizard. "The tail has the best meat – in fact the only edible part." He continued talking as he sliced off the last three feet of the lizard's thick tail; "the rest of the body is contaminated with bacteria that could kill an Elephant." He threw the section of lizard meat over his shoulder and stood looking at Amelia. "What's your name, Miss? We never got properly introduced."

"Amelia," she answered with some apprehension, "Amelia Earhart."

"Nice to meet you Miss Earhart," the man replied – smiling again and shifting the weight of the lizard tail to his other shoulder. "You're welcome for dinner," he said, as his smile broadened, "my place is just a carriage ride away."

FIVE

Amelia weighed her options. She could follow this strange man to who knows where, or she could go back to the safety of the plane. *This man is the only human contact I've had,* she considered, *and he holds all of the answers. He knows about the island, and the various creatures that inhabit it. He evidently has some idea of where the island is located and its proximity to the closes country or continent. And, most of all, he evidently has learned to survive and stay healthy.*

"Why should I trust you?" she found herself asking.

"If trust is an issue, Miss," the man said with raised eyebrows, "then ain't that really a two way street – why should I trust you to not use that machete on the back of my neck – and why in mercy's name would I have saved your life if I meant to harm you?"

Amelia knew that the Australian man made sense but she was also trying to follow her best survival instincts. "Just tell me about yourself, and why you're here."

"The animal's hindquarters is becoming a burden Ms. Earhart," the man answered with a sigh; "Have I given you a reason to distrust me? I ask that you please simply follow me to my humble abode and I'll tell you a compelling story over a tasty dinner."

The man seemed sincere and he actually bordered on being charmingly amusing. Her instincts said to trust him but she was still reluctant. She shifted the weight of her pack as she leaned forward on her right foot, now completely pain free. "Knowing your name would be important if I'm to trust you."

"Jack Bailey," the man said as he turned to walk away. "If you're up for a stroll, Miss, and trust your womanly instincts, you just might actually enjoy my company," he continued talking without turning around.

She did trust her instincts and they were telling her that this man was probably okay and meant her no harm. "Who else lives on the island, Mr. Bailey," she shouted as she rushed to catch up – "what are the natives like?" Amelia waited for a reply but the man never turned to answer. She was amazed that her right foot now felt perfectly fine – no pain or swelling. The cut on her head seemed to also be healed. She had no idea of what to attribute the miracle healing to but she didn't have time to think about it now – Jack Bailey moved through the jungle like a sleek panther, quickly following a path he evidently knew by heart and had traced many times before.

"Glad you decided to join me, Ms. Earhart," he finally shouted back with a laugh, "We'll soon see who has the best 'cast away' story."

Amelia was determined to keep up with her rescuer and was soon only steps behind him. The two moved fast along the narrow path and said nothing for almost an hour. Finally, Jack stopped at a wall of dense foliage were the path died away to nothing. "Welcome to my humble home," he said as he turned to face Amelia's startled face.

"You live in the brush?"

Jack laughed; "Through the brush, Miss," he said as he maneuvered his way through a narrow crack in the foliage, "I keep my castle hidden from the evil knights."

Amelia hesitated.

"Are your positive instincts about me slipping a little?" Jack asked with a smile. "I can assure you, Ms. Earhart, that after entering the brush, you will once again hold me in your highest regard."

This man does have a way with words, Amelia thought. She'd come too far to turn around now, but as she followed through the opening in the brush, she instinctively placed her right hand on the handle of her machete.

"There are steps cut into the earth ahead, Miss, so watch your step."

The sun was high and Amelia knew that it was now past noon. The tall trees around her provided shade, blocking out a lot of the mid-day sunlight and bringing in cooler temperatures as the two proceeded down a narrow stairway. The steps were wide and easy to follow and continued down the hill at a gentle angle. Jack stopped again. He stood next to an archway of stone with the lizard tail still draped across his chest.

"The grand entrance into my meek habitat," he said as he stepped back to allow Amelia to enter the archway first. He removed his hat and bowed, beckoning her forward.

Amelia shook her head, but said nothing. She was determined to stay behind this man even though he had saved her life.

Jack smiled and nodded, "I realize that trust is a fragile commodity and needs to be earned, Ms. Earhart, I can understand that." He moved through the stone archway and stopped at a place that appeared to be a deck or balcony. Amelia came up from behind and stood beside him. He dropped the lizard tail on a nearby stone shelf and held his right hand out. "It's not much, but it's my home – it's all I have to offer."

What lay before her was almost too much to take in – A lost city of stone that stretched out into the jungle for hundreds of yards. She saw no end to the towers and parapets that extended upward. Snaking vines covered almost every vertical surface and tall palm trees lined what must have been crisscrossing causeways in another time. Beautiful white egrets flew in formation over the palm trees. She leaned forward against a stone rail that curved around the front of the balcony. She swallowed hard and took in a deep breath before attempting to speak. "This is where you live?" she finally managed to say.

"Since 1920, Ms. Earhart – since right after the end of the Great War."

She turned to Jack and reflected on the answer. "You've been here for seventeen years?"

The smiling man raised his eyebrows, "It *is* 1937, isn't it," he answered, "I've been keeping up with the passing of every day since I arrive and I never miss a day – I never lose count of the days and the weeks but I haven't added all of the years up. It's hard for me to think about the current time and year as 1937."

"You must have been very young when you came here," Amelia responded.

"I'll tell you the whole story when we get down below, but right now, this hunk of meat needs to be boiled, skewered and made ready for the barbie."

SIX

The jungle floor of the sprawling city was approximately

twenty feet below the balcony on which Amelia and Jack stood.

As they moved from the balcony, a series of winding steps took

them down to a terraced garden at the bottom of the basin. The

garden surrounded a single stone dwelling nestled among a grove

of tall palm trees. From that point, the stone city spread itself

outward and upward through the jungle – a dense canopy of trees

covering most of the ancient stone structures. Amelia could not

help but notice that the dwelling they approached seemed almost

new.

"I keep the house and garden up as I can, but it's a constant

fight with the jungle," Jack said as he stood at the doorway to his

house. A thin canopy made from sail cloth covered most of the

entrance and a huge iron pot sat at the edge of the patio next to the

garden. The big pot was full of water and a variety of tree limbs

and twigs were piled below its curved bottom. Jack hung the lizard tail on a hook suspended just above the pot and proceeded to light the fire under the iron kettle. "She'll be boiling shortly and our friend will take a swim. I'll only boil it long enough to cleanse it and cut it up, then it goes on the barbie for the final skewering. We've got a while to discuss our stories before dinner." Jack sat on a low stone wall next to the kettle and pulled out a weathered pipe from the rear pocket of his shorts. He pressed his thumb down into the opening and lit the contents of the pipe with the same long stick he had used to light the fire under the kettle. He sucked on the pipe until a few sparks immerged and a wisp of white smoke circled his head. "Don't mind do you, Miss?" he finally asked as he inhaled another draw and once again removed his hat.

Amelia shook her head slowly as if in a dream. She sat on the same stone wall a few feet away.

"Me and four of my mates ran a charter service in and around the Gulf of Carpentaria, mostly sailing to New Guinea," he started. "We concentrated on the deep-sea fishing trade, but sometimes we'd haul cargo and passengers. I had more experience at sea than the others so they voted me to be their captain. Our vessel was a fine one, salvaged from the war – steel hull, twin screw. At sixty-five feet she could handle most of the squalls that came up above the 8th parallel. We traveled all around Indonesia – Rinca, Bratby, and Flores – anywhere the fishing was good and the paying passengers wanted to go." Jack sucked on his pipe and stared off into a vivid memory that was etched in his mind. "The typhoon caught us all flat footed – winds squalling across our bow at 130 knots and waves as big as barns. We wrecked here in 1920 – Me and three of my mates made it out of the storm. Now I'm the only survivor."

Amelia was trying to grasp the meaning of this short story and her mind was full of questions. She feared that most of her questions might produce answers that she really wasn't prepared for, so she sat on the stone wall in silence and simply nodded in Jack's direction.

"Can you top that story, Ms. Earhart?" Jack asked as he stood and shook out the pipe, placing it back into his hip pocket. "You can tell me your adventure while I boil us up a lizard." Moving to the winch on the side of the metal tripod that held the tail, he began to lower the aft end of the lizard into the boiling water.

Jack looked back at his visitor and saw a frightened young lady. He left the long tail to boil and moved to where Amelia was sitting. "Would a spot of Brandy help, Miss?"

Amelia blinked, and nodded.

"I'll be back in a wink," Jack replied with a smile as he moved toward the front door of the stone house. He disappeared through the doorway.

"What am I doing here?" Amelia asked herself in a whisper; "This man has lied to me from the start. He can't be much older than I am – how could he have captained a large vessel over seventeen years ago?"

Was this man a German spy? Amelia thought, *maybe helping the Japanese?*

Jack came back through the doorway with a short beaker full of dark liquid. "This should clear the cobwebs a bit," he said handing over the glass.

Amelia took the glass and stared down at the shimmering liquid. It smelled like brandy but how could she be sure. She handed the glass back to Jack. "You go first," she said without hesitation, her face void of expression.

Jack's dark eyes narrowed a bit as he took the glass, then he burst out in loud laughter; "can't blame you, Ms. Earhart," he answered as he downed at least half the beaker's contents. "Do you even have one trusting bone in your small body, Miss?" Jack asked as he handed the glass back. "Please tell me, how can I be more sincere than I've already been?"

Amelia took in a deep breath and finished the rest of the brandy in one gulp. It was like the water she'd drank earlier, a warmth flowed trough her that made things better but also made things worse. "You've been lying to me, Mr. Bailey," she replied in a clear voice. "You must think me very naive to believe that you captained a large vessel at such a young age." Amelia was starting to feel the warmth from the brandy in her brain and she was also beginning to feel her anger growing for this man that had given her false hope. "How old are you, Mr. Bailey?" she snapped, "Tell me how old you are."

Jacks eyebrows went up. "Well, I do believe that I'm seeing another side to your sweet self, Miss, but I do understand your confusion. By my best calculations, I'm exactly 32 years of age."

Amelia's stern expression never faltered; "And exactly how old where you when you ship wrecked on this island?"

Jack sighed and understood he could not lie. He knew what was coming next. "I was exactly 32, Ms. Earhart."

Amelia threw the brandy glass against the stone floor. "Why are you doing this to me – why?"

Jack grabbed Amelia's arms below her shoulders and shouted two words. "The water!"

Amelia blinked and tried to comprehend.

"The water in the stream, Amelia, it cured your injuries."

The water must be the miracle, she thought, "but … but …"

"And it has caused me to never age," Jack interrupted, relaxing his grip. "I'll be 32 forever, Ms. Earhart, because that water not only heals but it stops the aging process, and you'll always be the exact same age that you are now, unless you ever leave this island."

SEVEN

As Amelia picked at her meal of lizard tail, coconut bread and wild peas, she studied the rugged face of her host. She could see now that Jack Bailey was a strikingly handsome man. He certainly fit the description of a young Robinson Crusoe, and his blue eyes reflected a life filled with adventure and more than occasional danger. Amelia had told him the complete story about the proposed trip around the world, and about her other previous aviation feats and heroic accomplishments. She told him about Fred and the lizard in the cockpit and she also told him about her husband back in the states.

Jack had just started on his second helping of lizard when Amelia finished her story, took in a deep breath and sat quietly. She looked at Jack as if to say, *that's all there is, there is no more.*

"I do believe your story has mine beat, Miss," Jack finally said in total awe as he cut off more meat from the lizard's tail. "You a pilot," he said as he smiled and shook his head, "never knew a

Sheila … uh, never knew a lady pilot," he added, "I'd like to see this twin engine mono-plane of yours."

"The Electra!" Amelia suddenly said as she stood. "I need to get back – I never intended to stay this long. I need to get back to my plane."

The sun was dropping rapidly in the west and was not far from melting into the nearby ocean's surface.

Jack also stood. "You'll never find you're way back by yourself, Ms. Earhart," he protested, "wait until the morning's sun and I'll guide you back.

Amelia looked around Jack's stone house and thought about the possibility of sleeping there, and didn't like the idea.

Seeing her displeasure, Jack quickly added, "I have a storage room over the main floor, Ms. Earhart, and you are welcome to sleep down here and I'll take the bunk in the storage room upstairs."

Amelia knew the danger of trying to return to the plane by herself, but she was also extremely apprehensive about staying over night in Jack's small house.

"Can you take me back now?" Amelia asked, "Can you take me back to the stream where we met ... right now? I can find my way to the plane from there."

"It will be completely dark soon, Ms. Earhart," Jack argued, "but If you want to leave now, then let me take you all the way back to your plane. Leaving you at that body of water would be too dangerous. The stream is a watering hole for not only the island's lizards, but for several other dangerous creatures that lurk about."

Amelia thought about the offer and finally nodded her agreement. The two left the stone house and climbed back up the hillside stairway until they once again stood together on the balcony overlooking the lost city. Jack turned and proceeded back through the opening into the brush; Amelia followed Jack again, only closer than she had before.

As they started off, back tracking through the jungle, Amelia closed in on Jack and began asking questions she'd never gotten answers for. "You never told me about the natives of the island. What happened to the people that inhabited the city, Mr. Bailey?" she asked as she pulled up directly behind the fast-moving figure in front of her.

Jack slowed, and turned; "I wish I knew that answer, Ms. Earhart. I wonder about their demise every day, myself." He suddenly stopped and stood in place as he continued – "an entire civilization wiped out by something sinister – but what? The question has haunted me for over seventeen years."

"You've never found another living soul since you've been here?"

"In my seventeen years here, I've explored nearly every square mile of the island west, north and south of the basin. I've found no sign of human life on any of my quests."

"What about east – what's east of the basin?" Amelia asked.

"Jungle's too deep to penetrate," Jack answered with a frown, "one of my crew mates ventured that way when we first arrived here – he never came back. The jungle east of here is better left to itself." Jack took in a deep breath. "All of the people that once prospered here have simply vanished," he said as he turned from Amelia and stared into the jungle – "they've all just simply vanished."

"An illness," Amelia responded, staring in the same direction, "possibly a plague?"

"But they had the water," Jack answered, turning back, "that's the problem, they had the life giving water – why weren't they saved?"

Amelia noticed a vacant look in Jack's face, and the spark of his vibrant eyes seemed to be fading. She could see that her rescuer was pondering an unanswerable question.

The sun was dropping lower as Jack turned back to the trail, "we'd best keep moving, Ms. Earhart."

Back on the trail, they reached the stream just as the sun was fading away and dusk took the final light from the sky. "The plane's not far," Amelia said as she stepped in front of Jack. "I can make it from here."

Jack looked dejected as he protested. "You agreed that I'd accompany you to your plane," he argued, "there are dangers lurking between you and the beach that you can't even imagine, Ms. Earhart – things in the jungle every bit as dangerous as our lizard friend. Just let me join you as far as your aircraft, then I'll return to the basin."

"Really, I can take care of myself, Mr. Bailey," Amelia said firmly as she reached to her belt and gripped the handle of her machete. Felling a tinge of guilt about rejecting Jack's offer to be her body guard, she pointed in the direction of the plane. "If you want to come around in the morning, I'll show you the Electra. I'll cut a path from here that you can follow."

Jack could see that there would be no arguing with this head-strong woman. "So be it, Ms. Earhart, but if you get eaten alive during your journey back to your aircraft, remember your old friend Jack Bailey had issued you a proper warning." He took his battered leather hat from his head and placed it on his chest, yelling at Amelia as she disappeared into the thick brush; "But I'll be sure to give you a proper burial, Miss."

EIGHT

Amelia could not help but smile as she proceeded toward the plane. *The man does have a way with words,* she thought to herself.

The sounds of the jungle seemed amplified. Dusk had turned to darkness and she had the flashlight turned on now. Fanning its wide beam across the trail, Amelia thought she saw the reflection of yellow and red eyes along both dark sides of the path. Besides the great lizard, she wondered what other dangerous creatures called the uncharted island their home. An earth-shattering roar suddenly erupted from the jungle.

Amelia froze in her tracks as she withdrew the machete. She could hear and smell the nearby ocean and she knew the beach was close. She turned her flashlight off for fear of attracting the creature with the blood curdling roar. As her eyes adjusted to the darkness, she could barely make out the silhouette of her plane in the distance. Then she heard the roar again, only closer. Holding the machete in one hand and the flashlight in the other, Amelia decided to make a run for it. She had gone only a few steps through the jungle before she fell. She heard the sound of shrubs and bushes being trampled and crushed behind her. Realizing that something sinister was tracking her down and not far behind, she quickly turned the flashlight on and jumped to her feet. She didn't look back as she aimed the beam of the flashlight forward and ran through the palm grove that held her plane captive. Amelia reached the rear door and fell inside the fuselage, closing and locking the latch behind her. There was a jolt near the forward section of the plane, then a scraping sound across the top of the fuselage. Amelia realized that something was crawling across the top of the aircraft. She looked up and saw that several of the overhead insulation panels had fallen away, exposing the curved ribs and bare underside of the aircraft's aluminum skin. She then saw the thin metal skin of the fuselage buckle inward, as more and more pressure was applied from something outside.

It's trying to get inside the plane! Amelia thought as she slid into a corner of the small radio room and ducked under Fred's work table. She realized that she was still wearing her pack and remembered the flare gun. "All animals are afraid of fire," she told herself in a whisper as she grasped the pistol by its narrow grip. Sweat rolled down her face and into her eyes as she brought the gun up. She had six 12-gauge flares, total, and she could not afford to waist a single one. Amelia decided that she'd only fire the flare in defense if the beast actually broke through the skin of the plane. Then she remembered the broken windscreen on the left side of the cockpit. "It could come through the cockpit window!" She whispered in a panic.

The loud sound at the forward end of the plane sounded like an explosion; followed immediately by a vibrating roar that made Amelia close her eyes.

"It's gotten into the cockpit!" she shouted, not worrying anymore about being heard.

Amelia now held the flare gun with both hands and waited for the beast to slither aft – to come after her as she hid behind a bulkhead at the stern of the plane. She remembered the distance between the top of the fuselage fuel tanks and the plane's curved ceiling. She had crawled trough that low tunnel many times before and remembered the twenty-four inches of clear space. *Maybe It won't be able to get through*, she prayed.

There was another tremendous roar and the plane rocked again. Amelia held tight to the flare gun. Then there was an unnerving silence that washed over the dark interior of the plane. She heard nothing outside but was afraid to venture a look over the fuel tanks to the cockpit. Her heart thumped in her chest and she sucked in a deep breath. *Maybe the thing had left*, she thought, *gone back to the jungle*. As she began to relax, she sat down once again on the aft deck of the plane. She let her tired body collapse against the aircraft's rear bulkhead. Totally exhausted, she thought about her experiences of the last week. Amelia's eyes became heavy and her chin dropped. A barrage of whirling thoughts consumed her brain. *I crashed – Fred is dead – I meet a strange man that claims to be a castaway from Australia – I drank water from a jungle stream that heals my injuries and could possibly make me immortal.* She opened her blurry eyes and tried to comprehend the dreamy thoughts. Her head bobbed as Amelia fell into a deep sleep. The last thing she remembered was the water – *did it really cure me – could it really make me live forever?*

NINE

Jack followed the tramped down path that led from the creek that Amelia had cleared for him. *This woman,* he thought, *without a doubt, had been the most intriguing female he'd ever met,* but as much as he wanted to, he was having a hard time believing her story. Now, he was excited and anxious to see this aircraft that supposedly flew her almost around the globe.

It wasn't long before Jack stood in the palm groove that surrounded Amelia's wrecked plane. The sun was in his face and he had to squint to see past the trunks of the swaying palms but he easily spotted the silver silhouette of the downed aircraft. He was in awe at the size of the plane and its sleek mono-wing design. He knew nothing about aluminum so its silver skin baffled him, he had never seen a fabric covered airplane with smooth silver skin. As Jack walked around the wrecked fuselage he could see considerable damage to the forward section of the plane; "Her bow has taken a brutal beating," he said out loud as he stood among the palms. The cockpit seemed to be totally demolished and pieces of the interior were scattered about the jungle floor. *How could anyone in that cockpit have survived this crash*, he thought. Jack proceeded along the port side of the plane, the side closest to the whispering surf and spotted the closed door. He knocked lightly on the metal door with the end of his bow. He stood back, waiting for an answer.

There were only two windows in the rear of the plane and one was a small porthole at the top of the curved door. Amelia heard the tapping but could not see through the heavily crazed Plexiglas porthole. She could see a blur of movement outside but no detail. Amelia prayed that Jack was causing the blur. Slowly lowering the lever on the inside of the door, she unlocked the latch and pushed the door open. She stared through the narrow crack into the brightness outside. Jack Bailey stood just a few feet away with his hat in his hand and a smile on his face.

"Good morning, Miss," he said through the smile, "I reckon your story has definitely got mine beat; I've never in my life seen an aircraft like this one,"

Amelia pushed the door open as far as she could and stepped into the sunlight. She knew that she must look like a street beggar but she wasn't concerned about her appearance. "Good morning, Jack," she managed to squeak out, but she really wanted to wrap her arms around his neck and say; *Thank God you're here!*

Jack could see the circles under Amelia's eyes and her wild, matted hair. His eyes focused on her appearance with concern as he placed his hat back on his head; "Bad night, Miss?"

Amelia sucked in a breath and rubbed her eyes. "Something tried to kill me."

"Well, Miss, I told you that might happen, what else kept you up?"

Amelia was in no mood for Jack's jokes, or his cavalier, carefree attitude. Without smiling, she moved away from the aircraft. She lowered her head and looked down at the coarse sand.

"I'm at a place in my life where I never thought I'd be," she said, turning back to Jack. "A place where science and fact has been thrown overboard – A place where monsters dwell and a simple sip of water becomes poison in reverse – a liquid cure for everything – no more pain; no more suffering – life forever is your reward."

Jack took a step closer to Amelia, his face becoming serious, showing real concern. "Your having a problem with all this, aren't you, Miss?"

"Fred is dead and you're telling me that everyone else on the island is dead, why am I still alive – for what purpose have I been spared?" She ran the back of her hand across her nose and tried to sniff back her tears as her troubled eyes glistened with uncertainty.

"Oh, Ms. Earhart," Jack responded with a frown, "it genuinely pains my heart to see you this way." He took a few steps closer. "I felt the same way after all my mates passed … why was I the only one left?" He wanted to reach out to her, but he hesitated. "We've all been dealt a special hand in life, Miss. Some blokes have to stumble along on a pair of deuces and some step up in life